O9-BTI-961

Chill Wind

Janet McDonald

Frances Foster Books

Farrar, Straus and Giroux New York

Library of Congress Cataloging-in-Publication Data
McDonald, Janet.
    Chill wind / Janet McDonald.
        p.   cm.
    Summary: Afraid that she will have nowhere to go when her
welfare checks are stopped, nineteen-year-old high school dropout
Aisha tries to figure out how she can support herself and her two
young children in New York City.
    ISBN 0-374-39958-1
    [1. Teenage mothers—Fiction.   2. African Americans—Fiction.
3. Public welfare—Fiction.   4. Mothers and daughters—Fiction.
5. New York (City)—Fiction.]   I. Title.

PZ7.M4784178 Ch 2002
[Fic]—dc21
                                                          2001054785

To those who vanished on a bright blue September morning and those who mourn them, to my fellow New Yorkers holding their heads above water and their hearts above darkness, and to the Twins that tower still in our inner landscape.

Acknowledgments

For their contributions to the creation and creator of this novel, I thank word wizard Frances Foster and her skillful assistant, Janine O'Malley; Charlotte Sheedy, agent and friend; Madame Colette Modiano, Parisian inspiration; Paulette Constantino, Brooklyn buddy and reader; Annie Gleason, kin and critic; and Gwen Wock, partner in rhyme and literary compass.

Chill Wind

one

Aisha stood in the middle of her room holding the letter, spacing out. She could hear her mother Louise laughing at something on television, no doubt stretched out on her bed as usual. It seemed like ages ago that her mother worked in a laundromat, washing and folding clothes. Something else seemed like ages ago too. Aisha remembered dissin' her best friend Raven, also a dropout and teen mother, for wanting to make something of herself. She'd advised Raven to "chill," like she was doing, and just let the system take care of her. Now Raven's words came back like an ice cube dropped down her blouse. "I don't want to be like *you*. Anyway, nowadays they kick you off welfare after five years. So you won't be *chillin'* for long."

Two years later Raven was a sophomore in college engaged to her son's father, and Aisha was a nineteen-year-old mother of two holding a "60-Day Notice of Benefits Termination." Aisha's daughter, Starlett, had just turned four, and little Ty was barely two. Her mother Louise had warned her about making babies "with nothing coming in," and her so-called man Kevin seemed to think promises bought food and clothes for their kids. Her part of the rent was due at the end of the month, and the last thing Aisha wanted to hear about was her workfare options—scrubbing graffiti off city-owned property, working with the city's Clean Sweep Team, or joining the Zero-Tolerance Subway Youth Patrol—all for some piddling, temporary "transition" allowance. Raven's words came back again: *"They kick you off welfare after five years."* What was she going to do? With no diploma, no skills, and two kids, Aisha Ingram's chilled life had suddenly gotten a little too chilly.

Unlike her friends who had some kind of reason to leave school—usually pregnancy for the girls and prison for the boys—Aisha had cut short her education out of simple boredom. "I woulda bailed outta kinnygarden if they ain't had them def cookies," she liked to joke. As for one day maybe going back to school, she'd say, "Ain't took to it then, cain't take to it now."

Before motherhood, Aisha's life was all about being out. Chilling out, hanging out, making out, or just bugging out. And Kevin Vinker, a long-waisted mama's boy with big eyes and hair cut in a fade, was always at her side. Aisha lay back on her queen-size bed and remembered the good ol' days with Kevin, before Starlett and Ty came on the scene.

———

"Wassup, Miss Ingram. Ai home? We s'pose to be going to Coney Island." Kevin's untied burgundy sneakers were the same color as his loose-fitting jeans and backward cap, gifts from his mother, a subway station supervisor.

Aisha's mother, whose head reached the boy's shoulder, was dressed for work in a grayish smock adorned with rows of washed-out flowers and an assortment of stains. She squinted to bring Kevin into focus, a beer already in her hand.

"Coney Island?! She too sick to go to school, but she can go running way 'cross Brooklyn to some Coney Island? That girl as useless as her bonehead father, and I done washed my hands of her mess. And what about you, playing hooky all the time like there no tomorrow. Y'all think you know better than grown folks, but mark my words, you gonna end up just like me, making next to nothing in some oven-hot laundrymat washing folk's stank drawers."

Stank drawers. Kevin laughed hard at that one. Miss Ingram was a trip. And mad tipsy that early.

"Now move your narrow behind out my way, before you make me late to the office. That girl's back there in her room with a hot-water bottle propped on her head like she fooling somebody. I wasn't born yesterday." She hollered down the hallway, "And no, I can't loan nobody a dime!" and hustled off down the stairs mumbling, "They need to fix these broke-down elevators, like folk ain't got nothing better to do with they legs than run up and down steps."

One after the other, Louise had had three children with

her husband Louis, all of them, in her words, "good-for-nothings who can't send a dime to they mama." They were all grown when Aisha arrived, an unwelcome surprise. Louis wasn't any happier about the news and immediately announced that he was "done with being the mule" and was going to enjoy what was left of his life—alone. Soon after his wife got back from the hospital, he called for a gypsy cab to come get him and climbed in with four large trash bags stuffed with his belongings. For Louise and her new baby girl he left an "only for emergency" phone number scribbled on a brown scrap torn from a grocery store paper bag. That's when Louise began accepting Miss Barry's invitations to "come by and have a drink with a lonely old lady," and neighbors began whispering about how the Ingram family was going downhill. The Ingrams were actually two families: the one Aisha grew up in as an only child wondering where everybody went, with a mother who was often ill, cranky, or plain drunk, and the one her sister and twin brothers had been raised in by a playful mother and a hardworking father.

"Be careful at the fourth floor, Miss Ingram!" called Kevin behind her. "Somebody peed, and it's all wet." Still chuckling, he closed the apartment door behind him and hurried down the hallway to his girlfriend's room.

Two

Kevin found Aisha just the way Louise had described her, on the bed under a pink flowered bedspread, a red rubber bottle draped across her forehead. Plump but still shapely, Aisha was short like her mother. From Louis she got the round, smooth-skinned baby face that made her look more like Kevin's little sister than his fifteen-year-old girlfriend. He knelt down and gave her a quick kiss on the lips.

"Wassup?"

"She gone?" asked Aisha in a whisper.

"Yeah, she *way* gone."

Aisha kicked off the covers and bounded out of bed fully dressed in tight Levi's jeans, a snug ribbed T-shirt, and dark blue Nike high-tops. "Thank the Lord, I'm free at last! Cyclone, here we come! I'm starving, though. Gotta get me some White Castle hamburgers. Remember that movie we went to where them white boys had a food fight with hamburgers? Those *had* to be from White Castle, 'cause they was little and square. What's cool about White Castle is that you can eat a lot of hamburgers without it really being that much, 'cause three of them probably equal one regular one. I hope you got money. You heard Louise yelling about not loaning me nothing."

Kevin leaned against her, kissing Aisha's neck. "Yeah, my moms hooked me up with a little cash. But don't you wanna hang here and chill awhile before we head out? That Cyclone ride ain't going nowhere without you, baby, as fine as you are."

Aisha's cheeks filled with a grin. She liked feeling loved by her man, but they hadn't been to Coney Island in two weeks. And for someone who was always washing her hands of stuff, Louise was steady sweating her—do your homework, go to school, why you ain't got no report card. Aisha needed to break wild, bust loose. Anyway, Kevin always wanted to mess around. He'd just have to wait.

"We gots plenty time for all that, Kev, with *your* fine self. But right now I just wanna get rowdy and bug *out*. You try living with Louise, with her getting on your case every two minutes, and *you'll* be bustin' out inside too." She kissed his cheek and grabbed his hand. "Let's ride in the front of the roller coaster again! I wanna drop straight down screaming my head off!"

Even though Mrs. Ingram had gone to work, Aisha and Kevin crept quietly into her room. They dragged the heavy bed away from the wall. Aisha squeezed her arm into the narrow space between the wall and the bed and pulled out a jingling black sock that was tied tight at the top. "Got it!" She undid the knot and dumped a handful of subway tokens onto the sheet. "Yesss! Two for you, two for me. No, make that three and three, since we stopping at White Castle."

"Man, that's cold, Ai," laughed Kevin, sticking the coins in his pocket, "robbing your own mom's tokens."

"Oh, like you don't be all up in your mama's pocketbook every chance you get even though she give you anything you want. Now, *that's* what's cold. The way I see it, our moms be putting us through so much drama, they *should* be paying us. Who asked to be born anyway?"

Kevin agreed. "That's word. Let's split. But gimme some of them luscious lips first."

They took advantage of the restaurant being empty for a change—it wasn't yet lunchtime—and downed a few hamburgers at the counter. Afterward they had a short walk to the subway, followed by a long wait. At last the train rattled into the station. Inside, there was standing room only. Shoving through the crowd that was pushing against them to get off, Aisha and Kevin quickly grabbed two seats.

"Brooklyn style," boasted Aisha, proud of their aggressive moves.

"In the house," smirked Kevin, adjusting his cap and opening his legs wide so nobody could squeeze into the seat next to him. They felt like everybody looked down on project people, so wherever they went, they made sure to *represent*, and get respect: By always getting a seat on a packed train, even if it meant snatching someone out of theirs. By never waiting on line to get into a movie but walking straight to the front, daring somebody to open they mouth. Sometimes representing led to arguments and fights, but that's just how it was. A project thing. Representing. Getting respect.

"I'm hungry again," said Aisha, eyeing the bag on Kevin's lap.

"How many, baby?" he asked.

Aisha held up three fingers. She'd already eaten three hamburgers at the restaurant and two on the platform while they were waiting for the train. Even if she had three more, that would still leave her with four for later.

"Baby, you sure can *eat*."

"And ya *know* dat, but my shape stay sweet."

"Word," said Kevin, pulling her closer.

The train reached Stillwell Avenue. "Ai, wake up. Ai! We here!" Aisha's head was resting on Kevin's shoulder. After finishing a jumbo-size orange soda and her last hamburger at the Parkside Avenue station, she had dozed off.

"What? Kev? Where we at?" She wiped the corner of her drooling mouth with the back of her hand.

"Coney Island, baby! You ready to play?!"

"What? Oh! And ya *know* dat."

They emerged from the darkened subway into the glinting sun. "I shoulda brought my shades," said Kevin, shielding his eyes with his hand. Outside, the ocean air was cool and reviving.

Aisha peered through half-closed eyes. The beach stretched up and down as far as she could see. Straight ahead spread the ocean, its moisture making far-off things look wavy. The sun hadn't warmed the water enough for swimming, so people strolled along its edge, pant legs rolled up high on their calves. A child was giggling neck deep in sand as her mother emptied overflowing shovels on top of her. A small group had gathered around a man holding up a large crab by its claw. The boardwalk was a paradise of junk-food stands hawking cotton candy, Nathan's Famous hot dogs, red candied apples, popcorn, taffy, potato knishes, onion rings, and fries. And from the thunderous Cyclone roller coaster, screams rang out across the beach.

The thought of being whipped, snatched, and dropped by Brooklyn's famous roller coaster with a stomach full of hamburgers didn't sound so great anymore. Aisha linked her arm through Kevin's.

"Kev, wanna chill under the boardwalk before we get on the rides?" She felt lazy and heavy and knew he'd jump at the chance to hang out on the shadowed sand.

"Sho nuff!"

Three

First went Aisha, then Kevin, ducking and crawling under the boardwalk. They didn't have a beach towel, so Kevin spread out sheets of newspaper he'd found in a nearby trash can. The paper tore as soon as Aisha sat down, but she didn't care, as long as the part under her head didn't split. No way was she going home with sand in her hair and listen to Louise go off about fast girls and illegitimate babies.

It was chilly under the boardwalk, the dark broken by narrow strips of light. They were in a secret place hidden from the bright walkway above that thumped to the sounds of people with nothing to hide. Kevin rolled on top of her. The paper tore again. Aisha felt under her head—that part was still okay. They lip-kissed and tongue-kissed and neck-kissed, murmuring and giggling. Music from boom boxes mixed with the cries of seagulls. Then somebody walking above sent a shower of fine sand through the slats, straight onto Aisha's forehead.

"Hey!" She heard the sound of feet hurrying away. "They got sand in my hair!" She peered up through the slats and yelled, "Scrub!"

Kevin's mind was elsewhere. "It's ah-ight, Ai, you still look good." He pulled at her arm. "Lay back down. You got me all wound up." Aisha was sitting up shaking her head. Sand was flying everywhere. She wore her carefully straightened hair in a ponytail in back, with a bang in the front. And that bang had gone from black to beige.

"I can't believe this! Now I'ma hafta wash and hot-comb my bang all over again. People make me sick! They *know* kids be up under here! Let's go, Kev, before a dog decide to take a dump up there." She scrambled to her feet. "Come *on!*"

Kevin grumbled, "Awww, man," and stood up, brushing sand from the butt and knees of his new Lees.

Aisha hurried over to the parking lot and stared at her bang in a car mirror, smacking it until it looked black again, like she was beating the dust out of an old sock. "That's better."

She heard the familiar screams from the roller coaster and looked toward the ride. "Ooooo, hurry up, Kev, the Cyclone line is still short!"

They bought tickets and raced to the front car. The attendant, a lanky teenager wearing a black head scarf and dangling pants, gave Aisha a long look as he clamped the metal safety bar across her lap. "Don't be standin' up or ackin' all crazy," he warned, " 'cause I seen peeps in this front car go flyin'."

Aisha smiled big with her head tilted and eyebrows raised, a pose she felt made her look extra cute. "I'll be fine. I got me some angel wings."

The attendant rubbed the patch of stubble sprouting on his otherwise smooth chin. "You fine, all right, that's word."

"Yo son, why you gotta play yaself? You see she with *me*, right, so why don't you just go about your little clamping business before *you* go flyin'."

"I ain'tcha son," said the kid, easing away.

Aisha took Kevin's hand in hers. If a boy was ready to throw down for you, that meant he really loved you. She smiled at the thought.

Kevin tucked his baseball cap securely under his thigh. The roller coaster jerked forward and crept up the metal track. It stayed at the top just long enough for a quick view of the vast ocean and miniature people below, then plunged in a headlong, breathtaking rattle straight for the ground.

Aisha was screaming, the wind whistling in her ears, whipping the last grains of sand out of her hair and pulling tears from her eyes. Kevin shouted out as the ride yanked and climbed and dropped, his cries competing with the rattle and thunder of metal on metal. With each drop of her stomach, race of her heart, and squeeze of Kevin's hand, Aisha felt like she just might go flying. She was young, fine, loved, and free. Nothing could bring her down from the joyful peak where she hovered, not family, not school, not nothing.

"A buck and a half to ride some more, or leave your car and hit the door!" repeated the attendant as he moved from car to car collecting money.

A skinny black woman with a short 'fro stepped crying from one of the middle cars. A white woman was holding her up, repeating, "You're okay, Boo." The Asian couple in the second car were laughing and talking excitedly, waving dollar bills at the attendant. In the rear car, a black man in a PUBLIC ENEMY T-shirt was on his feet with both fists in the air, shouting, "Yeah, boyee!"

Kevin could hardly get his cap back on. "Whew, baby, *my* knees are weak, and *I'm* a man! You must be shaking through and through! No more Cyclone for me."

"Aw, come on, one more time, Kev! I love that ride! It feel like you really be in a cyclone getting all throwed around like—who was that girl with the poodle dog, you know, in *The Wizzid from Oz*, what was her name? Dorothy! Let's go again, Kevin, don't be a Herb!" Kevin said he wasn't no Herb, he just didn't want to ride no more. He offered her money to go up alone, but she sucked her teeth loud.

"That ain't no fun, you Herb. Okay, then let's do the bump cars!"

Aisha descended on the Eldorado Auto Skooter battle-field like a soldier ready to charge. The flashing lights and blasting music in the darkened ride riled her spirit and roiled her blood. Grace Jones's sultry voice sang, "Roll up to the bumper, baby!" as rubber-rimmed blue, green, and red cars slammed, banged, and crashed around the center divider like crazed ladybugs.

Each time the house lights rose, Aisha's hand was up and waving a dollar before the "another bump, another buck" announcement was even finished. Ride after ride she waved her dollars, while outside a red-orange band of light softly unfurled at the horizon.

As the last rays of daylight withdrew from Coney Island, so did the sight-seeing tourists, strolling families, and hand-holding couples. In their place came lone women with wobbling hips, guys with beepers, and cops dangling guns and billy clubs. Multiple collisions had left Aisha with bruised shins and a sore neck, but she was thrilled.

Aisha and Kevin stood at the counter of Nathan's Famous in front of a spread of mustard-drenched hot dogs covered with sauerkraut, ketchup-soaked french fries, and king-size Cokes. " 'The freaks come out at night . . . the freaks come out at niiiight,' " sang Aisha, perfectly happy. Kevin laughed through a mouthful of food. A shirtless man with feet as black as shoes and sooty pants shuffled up to them, his hand outstretched and his eyes on their mountain of food.

"Ugh, get away!" hollered Aisha. "Police!"

A dark-haired cop appeared holding a paper coffee cup in one hand and his hat in the other. "Move it, buddy! How many times I gotta chase you outta here? You disturbing the clientele. Come on, take a hike!" He ushered the derelict out onto the street, nodded at Aisha, and resumed his watch in the doorway, still sipping coffee.

"Hey, did you check out the name on his badge, Ai? It said Don Lennon. Like that hippie singer."

"Yeah, I remember him, the one they shot over near Central Park. But why you all in the cop's badge like you gonna report him or something? He was cool, saving us from that dirtbag after our food."

"Oh, it's just a habit. My moms got me trained from when I was little. She be like, 'Kev, if a cop say anything to you, don't talk back smart or nothing, but make sure you memorize his name so if something happen.' Same thing with car plates. In case I get knocked down in a hit-and-run. Like I would even be able to see license plates being all broke up under a car. You know how moms be, worrying about us. I guess that's they job."

"Not mine. Louise be like, 'If one of them cops out there catch you running the streets on a school day and whip your tail, I'ma go to the station myself and shake the man hand.' "

"Your moms is a trip and a half. Anyway, so what you wanna do now? We could listen to music at my place. Mines won't be home, she doing some overtime."

That was good news. The last thing Aisha needed was to run into Mrs. Vinker, who couldn't stand her or any girl Kevin had ever hung with. Just her luck to go out with an only child, and an only *boy* on top of that. Every only boy-child she knew had a pain-in-the-butt mother who wanted to keep him all to herself.

"Okay. I'll call home and say the train broke down and I'ma be late. You got a quarter?"

"Definitely!" he said, bringing his lips to Aisha's.

four

Kevin had sure been a lot of fun in those days. But as for school, Aisha could only stand it when she was bugging—like setting off the metal detector with her bracelets, shooting spitballs through straws, popping her gum loud in class, or making fun of girls in gym. Her alphabetically assigned seat was next to Raven's, whose last name was Jefferson, and they'd hung tight right through elementary, junior high, and part of high school.

Then Raven had a baby boy, got scared about the future, and ran off to some college way out in the boondocks where nobody could even visit her. It was a good thing her mother Gwen was cool and didn't mind looking after her grandchild while Raven was away. The day Louise did something that nice would be the day Aisha went back to school. Which she would never do. Even though she did have fun when she was there.

The husky teacher the kids mockingly called "Elvis" because of his name and sideburns spotted Aisha slipping into science class through the back door. She was very late as usual.

"Who can tell the class what the five senses are? Why don't you give it a try while you're here, Aisha, since we don't know when we might see you in class again."

Cackles.

"Why you gotta say that, Mr. Elveen? I was sick with the monthlies, and I even got a doctor note." Aisha was convinced she was good at doctor handwriting, even though her teachers never fell for it.

"Well, I guess we learn something new every day. I thought you girls got your periods once a month, not every *week*."

Louder cackles.

"What*ever*. Let me think, the five senses . . . umm, lend me fitty *cents*, ya mama ain't got no *sense*, the Bible say don't commit *sins*, and why go to school *since* we ain't getting good jobs nohow!"

The class burst into laughter. Raven laughed so much, tears were running down her face. Aisha looked around with pride like she'd correctly recited the name of every muscle and bone in the human body.

"That was only four, Aisha, but no matter—your grade just went from a D to an F."

"Then F *you*, Elvis. I hate your class anyway."

An angry Mr. Elveen leaped to his feet just as the bell rang, but Aisha was already gone.

The lunchroom was noisy. Trays bumped against trays, silverware clanked. Rows of tables and benches stretched from one end of the room to the other, prison style. Voices shouted out commands.

"Get me a milk while you up!"

"Ask the lady if they got any extra grilled cheese sandwiches!"

"Bring me two desserts! I'm holding your place!"

Students pushed trays along the food counter and piled them with sandwiches, milk, apples, and cupcakes. Using her big body and bigger attitude to shoo kids off, Aisha saved an entire table for her friends—Raven, Keeba and Teesha Washington, and Toya Larson.

"Grilled cheese again?!" complained Teesha. "Just 'cause the school get free government cheese don't mean we want to eat it *every* day. I needs variety in my diet, some fried baloney or chicken bresses or *something*." She took a bite of the sandwich.

"What you mean? You already *got* chicken bresses," teased Aisha, pointing at Teesha's small breasts.

"Unh-unh, Ai, don't be making fun of my sister's bress buds, or I'ma hafta lay you out right here on this table— even though she *do* wear a size thirty-two thimble cup!" Keeba exploded into laughter so hard that other kids laughed just from hearing it. Teesha stabbed her thumb into the center of her sister's sandwich, leaving a buttery hole.

The girls ate, drank, and gossiped about who looked like she was trying to hide being pregnant and which knothead boy probably did it. Toya said the Bible teaches chastity until marriage.

"I believe in charity too, Redbone," laughed Aisha, using the nickname Toya got because she blushed like a white girl, "especially if he poor *and* cute."

Raven rolled her eyes. "Chastity, Aisha, chastity. Meaning staying a virgin, not putting out for the poor."

"Chadiddy, charity, whatever. All I'm saying is everybody s'pose to love one another, and since me and Kevin in love, that's what we do."

"Oh, please!" protested Toya. "Doing the nasty when you still a girl is not what that means. I just hope y'all using some kind of birth control, because ain't no turning back once you knocked up. Look at what happened to that girl Sarah Elly from home economics class. Where's her Jeffrey now? Gone on to the next hottie!"

"Listen up, Virgin Mary," smirked Aisha. "Boys don't like it if you be all like, 'Oh, baby, can you put this on first.' It break they concentration and cut off the feeling. At least, that's how Kevin is."

"You's a sucker born yesterday, Aisha," said Teesha, picking up the last crumbs of her grilled cheese on her fingertip. "Kevin just can't be bothered. If he was really trying to

look out for you instead of just getting some, he'd do it anyway, right, girls?"

"Right," agreed the girls in unison.

"Y'all just jealous 'cause your chicken bresses cain't get
you no man!"

"What?!" said Toya.

"I know you don't mean me!" said Keeba.

"You better look at the skank in the mirror!" said Teesha.

"Ya big mouth done done it now!" said Raven.

An apple core bounced off Aisha's chest, then a piece
of cupcake hit her on the nose. Within seconds, balled-up
napkins, chunks of bread crust, and bits of cheese were
raining down on her, amid screams and laughter and the
lunch lady yelling, "Girls! Girls!"

Gym class was scheduled after lunch so the students
could work off the calories they consumed in the cafeteria.
Aisha was still giggling to herself as she squeezed into her
gym suit. "I'ma get all of them. I'ma get 'em good." She
adjusted her pantyhose snugly inside her sweat socks. The
gym teacher said the girls were to wear socks only, but
Aisha refused, saying she couldn't exercise without pantyhose holding in her thighs.

Nobody understood why a professional hooky-player like
Aisha showed up regularly at the one class everyone hated
most—gym. Even Raven, who got "best attendance" in
every class, had to force herself to the weekly torture ses-

sion of circular arm movements, jogging, waist bends, and, worst of all, sit-ups.

Pat Black, a stocky Southern belle, told them her greatest love as a gym teacher was "whipping chunkies into shape." It seemed she also loved blowing the whistle that dangled from her neck, which she was doing when Aisha sauntered in, took a small board from the stack, and joined the "posture line-up."

"Are we all here? Let's go! Form two lines. Step right, step left, step right . . ."

Balancing the wood on their heads and holding their backs straight, two rows of ten girls each stepped right and left and right and left, from one end of the gym to the other. They were determined to do whatever it took to pass gym and not have to make it up during the hot summer months. A couple of boards hit the floor, causing curious heads to turn and dump more boards.

A sharp whistle stopped the march. "Girls, we are *not* watching other girls because we are *not* nosy. We are concentrating on holding our backs erect. Now step, and step, and step . . ."

Aisha whispered to Sandy's back, "Check out how far Marcia's butt sticks out . . . talk about 'baby got back,' she could deliver pizza on *that* tray."

Sandy, holding her head straight, cut a glance at Marcia. She made a sound like a muffled sneeze, clamped her hand over her mouth, and threw her head back laughing. Her board flew into Aisha's stomach, which doubled Aisha over with giggles that toppled *her* board to the floor and sent her to her knees to get it, which made the girl behind her look down and lose *her* board . . . By the time Miss Black had pierced every eardrum with her whistle, the whole class was in hysterics, picking up wooden boards.

"That is *enough*! Everybody get mats! You've all got so much energy, let's see you put it to use for a few sets of leg raises."

The room filled with moans, groans, and grunts. And that was before the first leg was even raised.

"I hate gym! Hate it, hate it, hate it," hissed one girl.

"My stomach so big, I can't see my legs, let alone lift them up," complained another.

"How's somebody s'pose to be able to raise both legs off the floor at the same time? I can slide my feet up to my behind, but that's *it*."

"Miss Black's crazy. I read in a magazine that leg raises are bad for your back. I better not get hurt, or I'm suing."

And so went the complaining and griping as girls crawled, sat, and rolled onto their backs on the thick green mats, all eyes on the gym's water-stained ceiling. Aisha made herself real comfortable, placing her hands behind her head as if relaxing at the beach. A shrill whistle marked the beginning of the count.

"This is hurting me!"

"I can't! My knees won't go up!"

"If my back break, Black getting whacked!"

Aisha was daydreaming about the times she was in that

same position snuggling up nice and close with Kevin. There was Prospect Park and the Coney Island boardwalk and his cousin's car and . . .

Miss Black's whistle screamed directly above her head. Aisha jolted upright.

"You scared the *mess* outta me with that whistle, Miss Black, what's *wrong* with you?! If I go deaf, this whole school in trouble!"

"Your ears are just fine, Aisha. What you need to worry about is that waistline of yours. Leg raises will tighten those abs up. You can do it. Lie down and give me your ankles. And what's with this outfit? You know you're not supposed to have on tights *and* socks."

She pushed Aisha's shoulders down onto the mat, squatted, gripped her ankles, and hoisted them up and down.

"There you go, Miss Ingram, you're doing leg raises. See, girls! You all *can* do it if you just make the effort. Now Aisha, try to hold your legs up when I let go, so you *really* work your stomach muscles."

The teacher released her hands, and Aisha cut loose a loud fart as her legs dropped down. Miss Black fell back onto her butt, grimacing.

"Sorry, ma'am," said Aisha in her best Southern accent, "must be dat dang gubmint cheese."

Long after she had dropped out of Benjamin Franklin High, students were still telling the story about Aisha's leg raises.

———

Aisha's early teenage life was in a pleasant groove. There were more trips with Kevin to Coney Island. Meaning more stops under and above the boardwalk, tumult on the Cyclone, and collisions at Eldorado. There was disruptive fun at school—that is, when Aisha went, which happened if she was in the mood to hang out or wanted a free lunch. Keeba and Teesha lived in her building and had friends over whenever Mrs. Washington was away doing ministry work. Aisha would party with them all night, dancing, singing, and occasionally making out with some other fine boy if Kevin wasn't around.

When the weather got warm, people set up huge speakers in the street and held block parties with home-cooked meals, dance contests, and occasional fistfights between drunken spouses. Aisha would put on her shoe skates and go zooming in a pack of speeding girls all around the neighborhood. Or she'd just kick it on the benches, gossiping, playing cards, and telling 'ya mama' jokes. Evenings, she chilled at home, eating and watching movies and TV sitcoms late into the night.

Other than Louise's outbursts about her being "just like bonehead Louis," Aisha had it made. Sure she'd have to settle down and get a job when she was older, but that was the future, and the future could wait. She was about one thing—having a good time. Something she did quite well. Until the good times ended abruptly that summer, when, still just fifteen, she got pregnant.

Aisha's mother was enraged. For hours and days and

weeks she ranted about stupid fast girls bringing illegitimate brats into the world and stupid lying boys without a pot to pee in. Her daughter's life seemed a world away from the one Louise Brown, a seventeen-year-old newly crowned Miss Teenage Schenectady, had lived in when she met Louis Ingram, a drummer in the pageant band.

When she was her daughter's age, Louise was petite, curvaceous, and dreamy with fantasies about the fabulous future that awaited her. She would go for the Miss Eastern New York pageant, then Miss New York State, maybe even Miss America. After those successes would come the commercials, modeling career, and movie stardom. The pretty daughter of the town's sanitation chief, "Lil' Lou" was popular and confident. There was no doubt she'd get as much of the world as she asked for, and Louise wanted it all. Beginning with Louis. Louise and Louis made a cute couple, and everybody called both of them "Lou." When former teen queen and pageant director Sara "Brown Eyes" Hill moved her operation to the next small town of starstruck young girls, the drummer stayed behind. All Louise knew about the tall, flirtatious musician was that he could make a drum sing. Back then that was enough. Now, her bonehead husband was just a bad memory—one Aisha felt her mother took out on her.

"Ain't you old enough to know that sooner or later every man starts barking?" Louise responded in disgust when Aisha broke the news about being pregnant.

"Kevin loves me."

"Please! Every boy say he love you until he get what he after. Do he love you enough to marry you? To hold down a job to support you? To stay home at night? Plenty fools out there bringing illegitimates into this world, but I never thought I'd raise one!"

But as Aisha's stomach grew larger, her mother's tirades got shorter, until finally Louise announced that she was washing her hands of all of it.

"And do not, I repeat, do not take me for no live-in babysitter. That child gon' be yours and yours alone—*you* responsible. Now you take your fast, unwed-mother tail over to that welfare office and sign up for food stamps and aid money. My little check can't stretch but so far."

Aisha knew Louise had her own problems. Drinking had taken its physical toll, and since getting on disability because of her high blood pressure, Louise mostly passed her days watching TV. But still, thought Aisha, she was gonna be a grandmother. At least she could *try* to act like it.

Kevin's reaction bothered Aisha the most.

"You sure it's mine?"

"No Kevin, it's Sanny Claus baby. Of *course* it's yours! Who else baby it gonna be? You know, you a trip, talking out your face about loving me and everything, then coming out your mouth like that when I tell you about our baby."

"Awww Ai, don't be like that, you know you my main squeeze. It's just that Qua-Qua cousin said you was hangin' around with this dude at Keeba's party, so I figure maybe—"

"What?! Who the hell's Qua-Qua's cousin? I know you don't mean that skinny-behind, gossipin' Shanet who been trying to get with you from day one! I'ma bust her up! Hey, we can do that DNN or whatever it is test they got *today* and settle this right here, right now."

"Nah man, we ain't gotta be doing all that, Ai. If it's mines, it's mines. That's cool."

Soon after that Kevin started dropping by less and calling on the phone more. He was busy getting things set up for them, he said, looking for a full-time gig. When Aisha called, his mother always picked up. "Not here." *Click.* Aisha wasn't about to let herself be played like that and stopped calling.

The grown-ups around her didn't seem very surprised by her pregnancy. It was as if they expected it. Girls were getting pregnant all over the projects. Nobody other than Louise even said "unwed mother" or "illegitimate" anymore. Aisha was normal. Of her friends, the ones without children were happy for her and helped pick out earrings and outfits to dress the baby up in. The young mothers gave her advice about good prenatal clinics, public assistance, dealing with labor pains, and where to sell food stamps for cash.

As the baby grew inside her, Aisha stayed inside more. Parties and boys, roller coasters and bump cars all faded into the past, along with her childhood. She gained weight and grew lonely. She yearned for the baby to come out just so she'd have company. And when she did appear, Starlett

Whitney, named for the singer Whitney Houston, stole not only her mother's youth but her heart as well.

Food stamps and assistance checks arrived every month, and the little baby became a little girl. Aisha played with her daughter, hung out with the other mothers, and saw Kevin now and again, even though things between them weren't like before.

Life resumed its easy, familiar rhythm. She had a pretty daughter, had left school for good, and got paid without having to work. Not bad. Ty arrived soon after Raven went off to college. Louise hassled her to get over to the caseworker and sign the baby up for benefits. And that was all she had to say about her second grandchild. So Aisha chilled. Up until she got the termination notice.

five

It was hot, and the elevator was stuck between floors. People who'd done their Saturday shopping weren't about to lug their bags up the stairs to their apartments, so they vied with the teens for bench space. Leafy trees bathed the side of the building in cool shade. Shrieking kids were whooshed along by strong currents of water bursting from open fire hydrants. Aisha, carrying a wide bag on her shoulder and maneuvering Ty's stroller, made her way to the bench and squeezed in between Toya and her father, taking care not to kick over their groceries. The Washingtons, like a pair of thick bookends, sat at each end of the bench.

"Wassup, Ai," said Keeba, sipping from a can of fruit punch.

"Wassup, Ty," said Teesha, drinking hers through a straw. She giggled. "I like that. Ai-Ty. Sound like Chinese food.

'An order of Ai-Ty with extra duck sauce, please.' Ha, that's funny, ain't it, Ty? Want some?" Teesha removed the straw and held the can to the baby's mouth. Red liquid rolled down his chin onto his light blue sweatshirt.

"See what you did, Teesha, with your clumsy self?!" Aisha snatched a towel from the baby bag and wiped Ty's chin.

Keeba leaned forward. "Yo, my sister don't need drama, so you best save it for ya mama. Why you so evil today? Got the curse? Oops, sorry, Mr. Larson," she laughed.

Toya sucked her teeth. "You so silly, Keeba."

Mr. Larson smiled. "I been married to Toya's mother for near going on twenty years. You think I don't know about the curse and napkins and tampons and all your other woman troubles?"

"Daddy!" Toya's face reddened.

Aisha sat forward a little and turned to Teesha.

"Sorry, Teesha. I got a notice from the welfare people, and it's buggin' me out. They trying to kick me and my kids off, saying my five years is up."

"Damn," exclaimed Teesha, "that's wak. The same thing happened to my aunt Neda last year. Welfare closed her case, and she ended up homeless."

"Don't be sayin' our aunt homeless, baked potatohead. They gave her one of them workfare jobs with the Parks Department, cutting down trees or mowing grass."

Teesha rolled her eyes. "Keeba, you way behind on your news. Aunt Neda quit after a week. That's why they said she

33

was noncooperating. I don't blame her for not wanting to be no Sheena of the Jungle. Keith from across the street said he saw her all dirty, curled up on the grass in Prospect Park."

"Lie!" yelled Keeba. "You lucky you at the other end of this bench, or I'd be upside your head. I'm asking Mommy soon as we upstairs. *Anyway*—Ai, they didn't offer you no job or nothin'?"

Mr. Larson said the city couldn't just drop people from the rolls. The state constitution said so. They had to give people welfare-to-work benefits, job training, or something. And if on account of being crazy or sick they couldn't work, the city had to keep paying their benefits. That was the law, he said.

Aisha made a face. "They offered me workfare all right. You know what I gotta choose from? Scrubbing, sweeping, and hassling. And not getting no real paycheck but chump change, and *that* only for a little while. It's terrible."

"What kind of jobs are *those*?" asked Toya.

"Slave jobs. I got the notice right here. I keeps it with the baby's diapers so my moms won't find it, since she ain't changed his diaper since he was born." Aisha read out loud, "Your workfare options are, one, City Buildings Graffiti Busters; two, Clean Sweep Team; three, Zero-Tolerance Subway Youth Patrol." She folded the notice. "I'm s'pose to let them know in two months, or I get kicked to the curb. Ain't that a lot of nothin'."

"It sure is, Aisha," said Mr. Larson. "But you might be in luck. They trying to get more women and minorities in construction. Maybe you could do one of our apprentice programs. It's hard work, but it sure pays better than pushing a broom down Jay Street."

Toya said it would be great if Aisha and her daddy worked together.

Aisha shook her head. She said even the thought of doing a physical job made her feel tired. "Thanks, but I'm barely five foot two, and I'm big, even though I lost a little weight after Ty was born. I *used* to be in good shape from skating and jumping rope before I had my kids, but like my moms say, all that's ancient history now."

Keeba had an idea. "Work with us. Me and Teesha are blowin' up like the Williams sisters, except we into hair instead of tennis." They stared hard at Toya, the competition.

"I don't know why you two are giving *me* the evil eye. Everybody knows my braids stay in longer than yours."

Teesha grunted. "Homegirl don't *think* so, Red. That's why they be calling you 'Toya and the Temples of Doom,' 'cause by the time you done tugged all hard, girls ain't got no hair left in they temples!"

"Word!" howled Keeba, holding her sides.

A faint smile tugged at Mr. Larson's lips.

Toya was bright red. "Umm-hmm, sure. That why now *I* do Val and Brigitte and a whole bunch of other girls who used to go to you. And you know what they call you two?

'The Robin Hoods,' because with your high prices y'all be robbing people in your own hood!" It was Toya's turn to laugh wildly.

Keeba yawned long and slow. "All I know is, the girls who come to us still got the hairlines they was born with."

Mr. Larson stepped in. "Enough ribbing and tearing each other down," he said. "You should support and encourage each other like those Williams girls. *That's* why they're successful."

Aisha didn't think braiding a few project heads in one building in Brooklyn was nowhere near as large as Venus and Serena was living. Besides, hair was not her thing. She wasn't breaking her fingers twisting naps and extensions for hours on end. She'd stopped wearing braids herself because her hair started breaking off at the sides.

"I can't spend my time fantasizing about rich tennis stars who already got it goin' on. I have to figure *my* stuff out, 'cause when it get real, you gotta deal. One thing is sure— I ain't taking *none* of those tired jobs. I'ma refuse, tell them I can't work. Who knows—me, Star, and Ty might just end up in the park with y'all's aunt." She forced a weak smile.

The evening air was soft. From a window high above, a voice called out, "The elevator work!" Toya and her father grabbed their grocery bags and hurried off. Keeba and Teesha got a game of boxball going, and Ty dozed. Aisha stared at the grass, its green deepened by the evening light. She thought of Aunt Neda curled up in the park.

Sit

The mail carrier in Aisha's neighborhood was never more popular than on the first of the month. That's when folks gathered in lobbies waiting for him like for the messiah. Having food, paying rent, or simply replacing a burnt-out bulb all depended on the timely delivery of Social Security and welfare checks. But folks had to make sure they got to their money before the mailbox thieves did, because the city took them on a hellish runaround before issuing a replacement.

Standing in her mother's dingy housecoat and nappy slippers, Aisha was waiting for both checks. How had a month slipped by so fast? She used to be excited and eager receiving her check and stamps, planning how she'd stretch it out over the month. Now all she felt was that this was the next-to-last check. Starlett was growing fast and would be starting school soon. Which meant money for clothes and supplies. Ty had a weight lifter's appetite and ran through disposable diapers like a waterfall. And Louise always had her lips pursed and hand out on check day. For the first time in her life, Aisha felt the squeeze of responsibility, and it was tight. She struggled to think up a way to hold on to the good life, keep the checks coming in. Then a great idea came to her.

Back upstairs, Aisha reached for the phone, even though she hated going anywhere near tacky Fort Crest Houses, a rival housing project.

"Yeah, hello, this Fort Crest Clinic? . . . Nurse Constantino there? . . . What you mean, what it in reference to? To me wanting to talk to her . . . Aisha. From Hillbrook . . . *Yes*, she know me."

Aisha could've smacked herself for not thinking of it before. That day on the bench, Mr. Larson had said benefits couldn't be cut off if you were crazy. She had checked the notice again. It said you had to get on workfare "unless you provide this office with documentation that you are ill, disabled or elderly." She listened to the clinic's "on hold" music, making crazy faces in the mirror. "Girl, you a mental disabled case, off the hook," she whispered to herself, "one ill nana."

A voice. "Hello? What? Hellooo!"

"Miss Constantino! I didn't know you was on the line! . . . Oh, that was just the TV . . . It *has* been a long time, two years, right? . . . They both doing real good. You should see how big Ty is, and he only two. Starlett gonna be in school in a few months . . . I'm ah-ight, I mean, I'm not ah-ight. I—I got a lot of problems and ain't been sleeping good. And sometimes I feel like, um . . . everything spinning around and making me crazy . . . Yeah, my mother know, and she real worried. That's why she made me call you, 'cause she want me to come in and get a checkup and maybe a note . . . I know you ain't no psychiatrist. Can't I just get a appointment? . . . Thanks. Okay, next Thursday . . . Yeah, three-thirty's good. Bye."

She hung up the phone. "Ma, can you watch the kids just for an hour next Thursday? Doctor's appointment!"

Louise didn't answer. But Aisha knew she'd baby-sit as long as it was about a clinic date and not about Aisha doing anything fun.

In the week before her appointment, Aisha applied herself with determination to the study of insanity. First, she paid a visit to Raven's mother and offered to watch Raven's son Smokey, only a few months older than her own little Ty.

"Smokey's at day care when I'm working—which you *know*, Aisha. If you're scheming to get to watch my new VCR, just ask." Aisha admitted that was the reason. Mrs. Jefferson said okay, "But no boy company!"

Next, Aisha went to the video store. She peered through three inches of barred, bulletproof window at a thin man with smooth, coffee-brown skin. Behind him were aisles of videotapes in boxes, beneath a large sign in red block letters: ABSOLUTELY NO PERSONAL CHECK OR FOOD STAMP VOUCHER. NO EXCEPTION.

"Yes, miss?"

"Y'all got movies about crazy people?"

The man laughed, showing bad teeth. "In America all movies about crazy people."

"That's word! But I want a movie with a girl who bug out, can't go to school, hold a job or nothin'."

He looked at her, shaking his head. "You American kids—why you want a movie like this? You can have and do and be anything in America. Why pollute the mind with nonsense?" He picked up a video from the counter. "A nice lady from down by the Brooklyn Heights just bring this back. Good movie. Good inspiration."

Aisha read the box. "*A Tree Grows in Brooklyn?* Unh-unh, I don't want no nature movie. I need girls buggin'."

Still shaking his head, he moved through the aisles scanning titles. He returned carrying a small stack. Aisha grinned and rubbed her hands together. "Lemme check 'em out." The selection was perfect. *Carrie*; *The Exorcist*; *The Breakfast Club*; *Heavenly Creatures*; *Girl, Interrupted*; and *Eve's Bayou*.

"Six video, two-fifty per video, that will be fifteen dollar for two-day rental, plus five dollar deposit, please."

A frown pushed the smile from Aisha's face. "Fifteen dollars, plus five—twenty dollars?! That make me *real* mad. Blockbuster got way cheaper prices than that, and you can keep they movies for three days."

"Then go to Blockbuster, miss."

Aisha made a loud teeth-sucking sound. "Y'all take food stamps?"

"Read sign, miss."

"I saw the damn sign. What's wrong with food stamps? They buy food just like cash do, right? I sure ain't gonna report you to the welfare. Please, mister, I need these movies."

He smiled broadly. "Okay. Twenty-five dollar in voucher."

They eyeballed each other for a moment, Aisha steaming, the store owner indifferent. She shoved the food stamps into the "pay here" slot, snatched the videos out of the metal tray, and left.

"Crazy Americans," he laughed, sliding the vouchers under the cash drawer with the others.

Aisha and her children spent the next two afternoons watching videos at the Jeffersons' apartment. Ty occupied himself hammering the floor with Smokey's toys. Starlett drew pictures of mommies, babies, horsies, and doggies with the bright crayons she was never without. And hour after hour Aisha watched girls tremble, puke, taunt, hallucinate, shriek, and weep while burning up classmates, battling Satan, harassing teachers, stoning mothers, fleeing mental hospitals, and plotting against fathers. A couple of times her imitations, complete with rolling eyes and loud snorts, made Ty cry and Starlett stare, reactions she saw as a good sign.

The Washington sisters dropped by to watch her rehearse being mental. With drooping head and blank eyes, Aisha answered the practice questions her friends assumed Nurse Constantino would ask.

Keeba began. "So Aisha, how are you, dear? Any problems?"

"Not doing good. Mixed up. Feel possessed."

"Like how you mean, Aisha?"

"Don't have no energy, and I feel things crawling on me, then it's like something evil's rumbling in my chest."

Teesha wasn't impressed. "Y'all corny. That ain't how you s'pose to do it, Ai—you just look like a druggie. You have to be freaky-deaky, buck-eyed, and nervous. *I'll* be the nurse. Good afternoon, Aisha. What be the trouble today?"

Aisha rocked back and forth, fluttering her fingers like she was playing piano, and did her version of Angelina Jolie in *Girl, Interrupted.* "I'm going nuts, Nurse Constantino, can't sleep or eat or nothing, just wanna run away, you know, free, but people be following me, and I can't go out so I'm climbing the walls, can't sit still, you follow me, nurse?"

The Washingtons clapped.

"Go girl, that was good!"

"You was mad bugged on that one, Ai. She gon' *have* to give you that letter if you pull it off like *that!*"

Aisha jumped up and down. "Yesss! Welfare ain't cuttin' off my cash, and ya *know* dat! I'm like that commercial for New Jersey, 'Me and Welfare—Perfect Together!' " The girls gave each other high fives. Aisha felt so confident that she did more impressions—Linda Blair cursing, Ally Sheedy chewing her cuticles, Kate Winslet swinging a rock. Not for practice—she felt ready—just for fun. The welfare people could clean sweep her behind! Aisha Ingram was keeping her benefits.

seven

Every chair along the wall in the prenatal unit was taken. Leaning against a cot opposite the vending machine, Aisha passed the time trying to guess who was having a girl and who was having a boy by how round and high the future mother's stomach was. The girls were winning, five to three. An intercom buzzed in English and Spanish with announcements about clinic hours, pages for doctors, and calls for blood bank donations. Aisha listened for Spanish words she recognized. She counted the number of candy bars in the vending machine, then the bags of chips, then the sodas. She picked off her nail polish.

A nurse's aide dragged over a metal chair. "Here, honey, you better sit down. How many months are you?" she asked, patting Aisha's belly.

"I ain't pregnant, thank you," snarled Aisha, rolling her eyes hard.

Another aide appeared with a clipboard and yelled in the corridor, "A. Ingram? A. Ingram!"

Jane Constantino had been a nurse for more than twenty years. She'd worked in the wards, the emergency room, intensive care, detox units, and labor and delivery. As far as teenage girls were concerned, there wasn't much she hadn't seen over the years, and she sensed immediately that Aisha Ingram was up to something. She just didn't know what.

"How ya doin', hon? You see I have a lot of girls waiting, so try to make it fast. Like I said on the phone, I'm no psychiatrist, but we do have one on call. You look good, by the way. I see you lost some of the weight you put on with the second pregnancy."

Not the reception Aisha was expecting. And what was up with the "make it fast" attitude? She was supposed to ask Aisha what was bothering her, why she needed an appointment, questions like that—not be all huffy about how many wenches was waiting in the hall. If she hadn't already had it two weeks ago, Aisha would've thought from her stomach cramps that her period was starting. She got so nervous, she forgot to droop her head down or wiggle her fingers or do any of the movements she'd been practicing.

"I gotta get free, I mean, bugs are crawling down my back, and men are following me."

"What? What men? What are you talking about, Aisha? Not for nothing, but if you're trying to get sedatives—"

"I ain't trying to get no—Nurse Constantino, I need your help, I can't eat nothing—"

"*That,*" she said, looking Aisha up and down, "I truly doubt."

"—and I'm going crazy and can't sleep and—"

"Listen, Aisha, you're a nice kid, but we *are* very busy today. Now stop busting my chops. What exactly do you want?"

Aisha hesitated, then decided to just go for it since Constantino was already giving major attitude.

"Nurse Constantino, I been feeling mental for the past few . . . well, since Ty was born, really, and I need me a letter for the welfare saying I can't work." There. She said it.

The nurse sighed and leaned back in her chair like a weary parent listening to yet another tall tale from her child. She took Aisha's hand in hers and looked her in the eyes.

"Hon, I been a nurse longer than you've been alive. Do you *truly* think you're the only girl to come see me because she'd rather stay home and watch TV than work? I'd love to be home too with my feet up, but nobody sends me a monthly check. So I have to deliver babies in order to be able to eat, pay the mortgage, and take my bird and two little dogs to the vet once a year." She sat forward and looked straight at Aisha. "You kids think you're so much smarter than everybody. I've had girls in here limping, high, spitting, what have you—all wanting the same thing. No, Aisha, I can't give you a note saying you're a nut job and can't work, because you're not. And you know what? The work-fare experience might be just what you need to begin to build a better life for yourself and your children. Now, can I get back to work before I end up collecting welfare too?" She rose heavily to her feet. "Give the kids a hug."

Luckily not a single Fort Crest girl—or boy—was outside when Aisha walked by on her way home. Otherwise she woulda broke wild on them. Back at Hillbrook Houses girls were jumping double-dutch on skinny legs and expert feet. Kids playing dodgeball were shrieking and weaving from the path of an oncoming basketball. Teens posing on banisters bobbed to music blasting from somebody's window. Women sat side by side on the bench, gossiping in hushed voices. Men returned home from day jobs as others left to work the night shift.

Aisha didn't stop to hang but instead went straight upstairs. She had no wisecrack answer when her mother said, "If that was a hour, I'm Oprah Winfrey." She checked on Ty, contentedly kicking in his playpen, and on Starlett, busy scribbling on a newspaper opened on the couch. Aisha went to her room, dropped on the bed, rolled onto her side, and cried.

By the time she got the second notice, the "30-Day Termination Reminder," Aisha had shaken off the clinic setback and come up with another plan. The way she saw it, back in the days when her mother was growing up, it seemed like girls had it better. A girl and boy dated for a while and, if they really liked each other, got engaged for a while longer. They married and found an apartment together, and the wife had babies and stayed home while the husband supported the family, which he *had* to do if he was a real man. Aisha liked the order and simplicity of that arrangement. Especially the part for the wife. And since she already had the babies, all she had to do to be a real wife was stay home and raise them, which is exactly what she wanted to do.

Nowadays things were wak. Wasn't nobody a wife or a husband since nobody got married. Everyone just kept living at home like they was still children, even if they *had* children. Unless they parents put them out and they had to go to a shelter to be robbed or beat every night. No, that wasn't for her. Aisha was about to become a very old-fashioned girl. And who to call on for help but her most old-fashioned friend, Toya Larson, the baby of the home-girls?

"Well, look who's stalking," joked Toya, running into Aisha at the Larsons' door. "I'd love to do your nappy head, Ai, but you know Mommy only lets me do hair on weekends so nothing interferes with school." She knocked at her door. "Mommy! It's me!"

Mrs. Larson looked through the peephole, unbolted three locks, and welcomed the girls in. She asked her daughter about her day, asked Aisha about her children, brought a tray of cookies and milk to Toya's room, and left the girls alone. As far as Aisha was concerned, Toya had the dream mother.

Toya also had a new computer. "Let me show you how it works, Ai, it's bomb!" Aisha said she didn't want to know nothing about no machine that didn't play CDs or movies.

"My computer does both! You can listen to a CD on it or watch a DVD movie!"

"Yeah, that's phat and all, but computer stuff gon' hafta wait. I wanna run a idea by you. You know I ain't been a virgin since Michael Jackson had his real nose, right? But I been thinking about maybe getting married in a church and settling down to bring up my kids like in a real family, you know, like your folks. Husband, wife, and kids. What you think?"

"Wow, congratulations, that's good news. Mommy always says that in this world a child with two parents is a blessed child. Even though most of our friends live with either one or the other, I think you have it better if you have both parents. The Bible says—"

Aisha cut her off. She wasn't in the mood for Bible talk. "Cool. So, here's the deal, you good in English and everything, so I thought you could do a letter to Kevin for me."

Toya looked confused. "Wait, wait, wait—hold up. If you two getting married, why're you writing letters to each other?"

"I ain't asked him yet, stupid, that's what the letter's for!"

Toya slid off her chair cracking up. "They getting married, and the groom doesn't even know about it! And she calls *me* stupid! Owww, my stomach hurt from laughing! Ouch!"

Aisha sneered at Toya, who'd turned red, then she laughed too.

"Go on, Redbone, bust out. But you *doin'* my letter. And when I'm all fly on the church steps in a white wedding gown with my husband Kevin at my side, I'ma aim my bouquet straight at your big, high yella moonface."

Before Aisha had even gotten out the word *bouquet*, Toya was rolling on the floor. "My stomach! Owww . . ."

Mrs. Vinker tossed the day's mail onto the kitchen table and fixed herself a cup of steaming coffee.

Where was her little boy? she wondered. Chasing behind that foolish-looking girl with the blond braids from Fort Crest, most likely. She raised the cup to her lips, and again she had to sit it back down. No matter how much milk she put in, her coffee always stayed too hot for too long. She lifted the cup and blew hard. "Oh, for crying out loud, look at this mess." As she dabbed a dish towel on the brown splatters that had wet the day's mail, an envelope caught her eye. "Strictly Private," it said. For Kevin? What could that be? Who'd be writing her baby? She picked it up.

It's not that Aisha expected him to write back. The scrub probably couldn't spell his own name, but he coulda picked up a telephone like a man. Toya's letter was *smokin'* too, good enough to make Aisha want to marry her *own* self. She had put in stuff from the Bible, from R. Kelly songs, from the movie *Love & Basketball.* Redbone had thrown down! Well, if Kevin was too much of a punk to call, then *she'd* be the man and call, and if his witch of a mother picked up, too bad.

"Kevin? Ai. Your moms's letting you answer the phone these days?"

"Yo wassup, Ai. She at work. You ah-ight? Been thinkin' about you. How Star and my little man?"

"They fine, but they miss they daddy. We ain't seen much of you lately. What you up to?"

"You know, just kickin' it."

"Oh, just kickin' it. So why didn't you just kick out a answer to my letter?"

"Letter? What letter? I didn't get no letter from you. I don't get mail. Anyway, my moms the one who check the box. You sure you wrote me? About what?"

That old . . . she stole Kevin's letter! Nothing to do now but ask him straight up.

"What I had wrote you about was that we been going out a long time and we got two kids together. Don't you think it's about time we got married and made a real family? We yours, after all."

"Whoa, slow down, Aisha, you goin' too fast for me. I'm still a young man, you know what I'm sayin', I ain't ready for no twentyfo'-seven daddy gig. I been tellin' you all along, when I'm hooked up right with a cash flow and my

51

own crib, then we all be hooked up. But right now it ain't happenin' for me. I'm stuck with my moms and—"

"Don't gimme that, Kevin. You *want* to be right where you are 'cause you ain't nothin' but a punk mama's boy who don't do nothin' but talk big with squat to back it up. You right, I *ain't* sure I wrote you. Matter of fact, I remember now, I didn't."

She slammed down the phone, hoping to bust Kevin's eardrum. Then she lay down on the couch and looked at the ceiling, seeing nothing, thinking nothing. Starlett walked over to her mother.

"Whatcha doing, Mommy?"

"Nothin', baby, just chillin'."

"Cuh I chill wichoo?"

"Yeah, baby, you can chill with Mommy." Starlett climbed into Aisha's lap and curled up against her stomach. Aisha held her close. She thought about Ty. They'd never be family to their so-called father, and she'd never be a wife to her so-called man. But they were still Ingrams. And Ingrams stuck together. She hoped.

eight

Mother and daughter chilled on the couch, the smallest of families. Aisha thought about Kevin not wanting to marry her, Nurse Constantino refusing to give her the letter, her welfare money coming to an end, and her own mother maybe putting her out. And there was the thought of sweeping the streets of Brooklyn. Nah, she wasn't going down like that—*something* had to break for her. She'd been barking up the wrong trees, that's all. It was time to turn to people who *couldn't* say no. She recognized the faces mainly from photos, but she had big hopes for the middle-aged strangers she knew as her brothers and sister. She picked up the phone and dialed her sister Ebony's number.

Ebony Ingram was born with attitude. She'd been a col-icky infant who cried and whined whether she was fed and diapered or not. In prekindergarten she pulled hair, slapped faces, and stomped on so many little toes that the teacher asked Mrs. Ingram to keep her daughter home "until she was ready to be socialized." Ebony's warrior temperament wasn't all her fault though. The youngest of three, she was forced early to go to war against twin brothers who enjoyed tormenting her in as many ways as they could imagine. Their favorites were jumping out of closets, growling under her bed at night, and putting scouring pads in her pillowcase.

The quick-tempered child never did get socialized. She battled her brothers when they teased her with the name "Ebonicky" and fought her classmates for no reason at all. She dropped out of junior high and dropped back in. She shoplifted makeup and graffiti-ed walls with her tag "Fly-chick." In church, she stole dollar bills out of the offering baskets and set fire to a pew. But what she did best was rebel against adults, especially the two struggling to raise her. And all of this, every last infraction, went completely unpunished because, with her father's height and her mother's looks, Ebony Ingram was absolutely gorgeous. Aisha had often wondered about her older sister, why she'd left home, how she lived, but Louise insisted that Ebony wanted nothing to do with them. Aisha decided to find out for herself.

"Hello, you've reached the Riordan residence. Leave a message after the beep, and we'll get back to you."

"Wassup, big sis, long time no smell, ha, ha. Gimme a shout when you get this message, okay? It's me, Ai, ya baby sister. Star wanna say hi. G'head Star, say wassup to Auntie

Ebbie. She too shy right now, but she miss you. Ah-ight, I'm out. Say wassup to Frank."

She placed the receiver in its cradle and picked it up again to try her brothers. It seemed dumb that her folks had given them the same name since it was hard enough to tell with twins who was who anyway. Perhaps it was because they themselves had been called Lou and Lou. Or maybe it was as Mr. Ingram had said, that the firstborn son always carries his dad's name, "like Martin Luther King Sr. and Martin Luther King Jr." Even if there *are* two of them.

Whatever the inspiration, Aisha's brothers were Louis Jr. and Luis Jr., the *o* being the only thing that kept teachers from going completely crazy. The identical boys loved to pretend to be each other or repeatedly enter a classroom one after the other. Their behavior made them regulars at the principal's office. The Lous were surprised and relieved that their sons managed to graduate high school, even if at the bottom of their class. The boys never married, choosing instead "a life of bachelor boys," as they put it. They spent a few years in California acting in "art films" that Louise could never find at any video store, and eventually returned to the East Coast.

Although they occasionally sent Aisha a joint birthday card from Florida where they worked with other handsome twins at Dino's Doubletake Take-Out, the only sister they knew was the one they'd grown up with. Listening to the phone ring, Aisha hoped that she could rate with them as much as Ebony did.

"You've found Lou and Lu, and you know what to do."

"Wassup, dawgs, long time no smell, ha, ha. Gimme a shout when you get this message, okay? It's me Ai, ya baby sister. Star wanna say hi. G'head Star, say wassup to your uncles. She too shy right now, but she miss y'all. Oh yeah, I got the card, thanks y'all. I'ma be twenty in June. Ah-ight, I'm out."

Louis Jr. and Luis Jr. had sent her a nice card when she turned nineteen, and last Christmas she got a scarf from Ebbie with a twenty in it. So the family feeling was definitely there for her—she just had to tap into it. Things were getting pressured, but she was on the case like a cop spraying Mace!

Aisha was dozing when she felt a tug. What the . . . Starlett was pulling on her hand.

"Mommy, wake up, Ty crying. Mommy! He crying."

Aisha shook herself awake.

"Thanks, honey," said Aisha, kissing Starlett's nose. She walked down the hallway, Starlett right behind her, the smell of beer stronger with each step.

"Girl, didn't you hear me calling you, you deaf? That baby in there screaming his head off."

Aisha hated how the drinking made Louise nasty. Wasn't it about time for her to pass out in front of the TV anyway? Her brothers might come through, or maybe Ebony. That would be bomb if she went to live with Ebony and Frank. They had a huge house in Queens with mad room and no kids. It'd probably be nice for them to have some life in they house, and she could take care of the place while they were at work, like live-in help. Not for good, of course, just temporary, until they got squared away. No more Louise sweating and stressing her.

"Then why you didn't get up and check on him? He *is* your grandchild!" Aisha shot back.

"Don't give me no lip, Aisha Ingram, or you can pack your junk and let the doorknob hit you in the backside. The pocket change you give me once a month don't even cover the milk that boy drink up in a week."

Aisha raised Ty's legs so Starlett could sprinkle him with baby powder, then she pressed down the sticky diaper strips. He gave them his best grin. Louise continued mumbling. Aisha got mad.

"Don't worry, Ma, we gonna be jettin' real soon over to live with my big sister if everything work out right, and you can bug out all by your lonesome—"

Louise's chortling turned into coughing, loud throat-clearing, and back to chortling. "*What* big sister?! Now I *know* you gone crazy. Ebbie taking you and them children in? Then my name Aretha Franklin! That girl wouldn't give the time of day to a blind man! Why you think she married that white man and moved way out to Queens? To get away from us, Aisha—you, me, your bonehead daddy, and everybody who remind her of this dump. Your *big sister* couldn't even wait for you to get used to your crib before she got outta here. Yeah, you go ahead and move in with Ebony and Irishman—and I'll shack up with Denzel Washington!"

She started cackling so hard again, she choked and had to down several swallows of beer.

The sounds made Starlett giggle. "Gramma funny!"

"*Whatever!*" yelled Aisha, hoping *so* bad her sister would call.

Days passed changing diapers, washing clothes, pushing the stroller, combing hair, ignoring her mother's mouth, and hanging at the checker tables playing cards. One particularly sticky day, all the girls were chilling in the shade. Teesha asked about the letter Aisha was supposed to have got saying she was bugged. Aisha told her it had to be from a real psychiatrist, not no common baby nurse. "And who got cash for *them* freaks?" she added, trying to play it off like she couldn't be bothered. Toya wanted to know about the wedding and was disappointed to hear that Aisha had changed her mind. "I don't want no scrub living off his mama. I'ma go find me a Tiger Woods." She looked at the ground. Keeba said Aisha be lucky if he even let her carry his golf sticks. So what was Aisha's plan? they wanted to know.

"My family hooking me up. Y'all know I got grown twin brothers and a grown sister?"

No, they didn't know, they said, but that was phat. Family was bond.

"So who got the cards?" asked Aisha, eager to change the subject from her problems. Teesha pulled out the deck of Rappers Delight playing cards she'd won by being caller number ten to 98 FM Rap Radio, and the first of several bruising games of knucks began. The first player out rapped the losers' knuckles with the whole deck, the number of hits equal to how many cards a player was left holding. By evening Teesha's knuckles were dark purple, and Toya had dropped out, complaining that Aisha hit too hard, like she was trying to kill somebody. Keeba promised both of them she'd get Aisha back but lost the very next game. Instead of holding out her fist like a good loser, she jumped up and went running.

The evening was heavy and humid. Upstairs, Aisha felt like she was suffocating. She put the kids to bed and looked in on her mother. Louise had dozed off fully clothed in her sitting chair. She turned off the TV and eased her mother's door shut. The phone rang.

"Yeah?"

"Hello, dahhh-ling."

"Hello, sweetheart," said a second voice. "I'm on the other phone."

Aisha was *not* in the mood. "This better not be no obscene phone call, 'cause I got Caller ID."

"Oh dear!"

"My word, did you hear that? Caller ID! The Ingrams have become ghetto fabulous."

"Who *is* this?" She was irritated.

"Don't you recognize the big brothers you miss so much that you called, when was it—last Thursday or . . ."

". . . was it Wednesday?"

"Louis! Luis! Wassup! Man, I'm glad it's y'all. I didn't even recognize y'all's voices."

"Girlfriend, you need to work . . . "

". . . on your English, honey, because you are too ebonics for me."

"And for me!"

Aisha's heart was beating hard. "Y'all still crazy!" she said. "So gimme the 411 on everything, how's work, how's Florida, when y'all getting married . . ."

Talking over one another, her brothers said, "Work—let's see . . . Dino's fine, he opened four more Doubletakes . . . San Francisco, L.A., Aspen, and where, where, where *is* the last one—oh, *Vermont* of all places. We're looking at Paris too. The French are into twins."

"And Luis, when are you getting married?" laughed Louis.

"When you do, bachelor boy," answered Luis.

"Paris? Whoa! Do y'all need a sexy waitress?"

"Yeah, Aisha, if you come with a twin."

"And heart-stopping abs, cut delts, and ripped biceps."

"I got all that! It's just under all my fat. So anyway, I called 'cause I might be getting cut off welfare—"

"Ohhh, the W word. Ugly, ugly."

"—and me and Star and Ty, we might need a place to stay, y'all know how Louise is . . . only for a few weeks max until I get a gig and my own crib. It could be fun for y'all, having family around."

Silence.

"Aisha, we wish we could . . ."

". . . but if you could see our place here . . ."

"To tell the truth, it's not even our place."

"That's right, we're in the guest apartment of Dino's condo."

"So I'm sure you see how awkward that could be."

"Yes, Ai, and Dino is positively allergic to children."

"Not that yours aren't gorgeous, because I know they are from the photos you sent, but . . ."

Silence.

"That's ah-ight . . . uh, I got some other things I'm checkin' out too. I mostly just wanted to give y'all a shoutout."

"Well, that is so sweet of you, l'il sis, and a shout back atcha!"

"Absolutely, Ai. And you *must* come visit us down here in the Keys. And bring Louise—she'd fit right in with the Hemingway crowd." Aisha's brothers chortled like school-boys.

"Okay, well—'bye, y'all. Star sleep now, but she said hi before. Don't f'git her birthday."

She listened for their click, then hung up too. That night, she had trouble falling asleep.

The next morning several brisk knocks rapped at the door.

"Ai! Don't you hear *nothin'*?!" yelled Louise from her room. "Ai, the door!"

Aisha groaned. She'd finally settled into a deep sleep and now was having trouble waking up.

"Ai! I *said* door!"

Aisha tugged at the housecoat bunched and tangled around her hips. "You got legs too!" She eased off the side of the bed and pulled the sheet over Starlett. She was dead tired. *Knock, knock.* Why couldn't Louise ever answer her own friggin' door? Hung over, probably. She slouched toward the door. *Knock, knock, knock, knock.* If that was them Jehovahs waking up the whole world this early, they was in for some drama.

"Wait!" she yelled in as mean a voice as she could, sliding open the peephole cover. She focused her eyes.

"Daddy?"

She hadn't seen her father for more than a year and felt excited even though she didn't want to. Maybe he'd— She swung the door open.

"What *you* doin' here?"

Louis Ingram had kept a little bit of the hip musician about him—the goatee and wide sideburns, the eyes yellowed by late hours in smoky clubs. But age was ushering him along, and he looked almost old. What hair was left on his head had grayed, his face looked jowly, his gut overhung the tool-laden belt he was wearing, and a slight stoop had replaced his strut.

"Look at Daddy's girl, big as a house! Give your old man a hug. You get my birthday card? They got me out here checking the valves on that new laundry room furnace Housing put in. Lil' Lou up?"

A few years back he started using Louise's old nickname, as if the teen beauty queen Lil' Lou was the only wife he wanted to remember. They had married on Lil' Lou's eighteenth birthday and moved into what was billed as a "spanking new public housing complex for Brooklyn's working families." Unemployed musicians, which is what he was at the time, need not apply, so Louis took a temporary job at the local utilities company so the couple would qualify for an apartment. Once they settled in he would return, or so he planned, to music, which was his passion. He was twenty years old.

Three years later the Ingrams were the parents of rowdy twin boys and a brash baby girl. Lil' Lou's formerly firm, tight body was showing the heft and wear of motherhood, and Louis had sold his drums. The temporary had become permanent. They were still happily in love back then and hadn't yet begun to blame each other and the children for their lost dreams and vanishing youth.

Aisha shook her head. "*No*, she ain't up—it's six in the morning! She back there crawling around on the floor looking for her lost head."

"Come on, Aisha, that's your mama, and she sick now so—"

"So why she gotta stay mad at *me*, I'm not the one who left—" She caught herself. A shadow crossed Lou's face.

"Be a sweet girl and go tell your mama I'm here, Ai. I gotta get back to work."

Still sleepy and yawning, Aisha checked out this man who

popped in and out of her life every few months. Or years. Whenever he was in the mood. He was her children's grandfather and her daddy, so why wasn't he being one? He brought them into this world, so he owed them *something*. And them few birthday cards with nothing in 'em but "happy" wasn't doing much to whittle down that debt.

"Daddy, it's funny you dropping by like this, 'cause I was gonna give you a call about a . . . situation. See, um, my welfare runnin' out—these days they put people off after five years, and I been on almost that long—so me and the kids gonna need a place. Mama don't want nobody up under her if they can't help out. I see where she comin' from and all, three *is* a lot—and, well, since you got a good job and living by yourself now . . ."

Mr. Ingram looked at his watch. "It's always 'Daddy, Daddy, Daddy' when you want something. Looka here, Aisha, I gave up my music and my best years taking care of you children and your mother, and I'm all gived out."

"But you never took care of *me*! You split soon as I was born, Daddy!"

"Oh, don't 'Daddy' me, girl. You just like ya mother back there, whining and wanting."

Louis Ingram did an about-face and was gone. Aisha turned and made her way to her room.

The sounds stirred Louise awake again. "Who that was?"

"Nobody. I'm going back to sleep." She crawled under the sheet and lay there wide awake.

nine

A full-bodied brunette tossed her wavy hair over her shoulder, planted both hands on her wide hips, and turned smoothly on the ball of her foot, smiling beautifully. *"Are you big, beautiful, and ready to live your dream?"* asked the cheery announcer. *"Then call us today at 1-800-BIGMODELS."* Aisha, munching a Hostess Sno Ball, propped herself on the Washingtons' oversize pillow.

"Keeba, could I get some milk?" The cupcakes always made her thirsty.

She sank her teeth into the pink coconut spongeball. Help hadn't come from nowhere, and the final countdown was now in weeks instead of months. Maybe her five-dollar Lotto ticket would win the $17 million or at least a few thousand for second place. She'd been too tired to jumble up birth dates, clothes sizes, and friends' apartment floor numbers and had let the machine pick the numbers. But she knew better. People always said the machines make you lose on purpose so the Lotto office don't have to pay. Whatever. Until she lost her benefits, she was going to enjoy life.

"Keeba!"

"I *heard* you the first time. Our milk don't go with them foam rubber pink things you eating. It go with Oreos." Keeba licked the white cream off the cookie she'd pried apart and took a drink from a plastic cup. She was home from school with stomach cramps—welcome news to Aisha, who never got to hang with her friends on school days. The good ol' days of everybody getting promoted even if they had bad grades were over. Now teachers were holding kids back left and right, even the ones who were really too old to still be in high school, like Keeba and her sister. And Keeba was cool about Star and Ty being there. Keeba's menstrual cramps were the highlight of Aisha's month.

The girls were deep into the afternoon soaps. As soon as Keeba put it down, Aisha snatched up the cup she'd just drunk from and gulped a mouthful of milk.

"Git outta my milk, pig!"

"Hmmm, don't they say milk is a natural?"

"If you put them greasy lips near my cup again, I'ma be a natural—a natural-born killer! Go get it out the 'frigerator, hog."

"Thank you so much, Robin Hood. Now don't it feel good to share? Hey, watch me do my model strut like that white lady." Aisha sashayed to the kitchen, hands on hips, head high. "I might just call them big models—I'm sure big enough." She returned to the bedroom with a milk container.

"Only problem, Ai, is big ain't enough. We *all* big. You gotta be cute too. Where your cup? No, you are *not* fixin' to drink out the carton! I swear, Ai, you put the *ghett* in *ghetto!*"

"Please, I ain't drinking out your booty milk carton. *Your* lips probably been on it. And don't worry about my looks. I take after my mama the beauty queen. Now *you*, that's another story. Ya mama so ugly, when she cry her tears go sideways."

"Don't start with me, Ai, 'cause you know Miss Ingram so ugly when she looked in the mirror, it broke."

The girls were suddenly nose to nose, wobbling their heads at each other.

"Right, Keeba. That's why *your* mama so ugly, the dog-catcher refused to pick her up."

"*Your* mama so ugly, she scared the *u* off the *gly.*"

"Now *that* was stupid, Keeba, just like you." Next thing they were pulling and giggling and punching at each other. Having run out of "ya mama so ugly" jokes, Aisha focused once again on her future.

"Ah-ight, jokes aside, I'ma call. Why not? Done tried everything else, right? I ain't letting nobody force me in one of them no-pay workfare jobs. If I gotta work, then I'ma be out there like Tyra Banks, getting *paid* Puffy style, I mean mega benjamins. I'ma travel all over, be all up in magazines and music videos like my girl Brandy, open me a bank account, take care of me and mines, chill, get another model job, count my cash, chill, and keep it goin' like that on and on and on."

"Well you go, Puff Mama, make 'em show you the money, I ain't mad atcha! I bet a lot of stuff that happen to folks is like Lotto—you can't win if you don't play. You probably *should* go for it. Maybe you right, something might break for you. But you *know* you gotta hook me up when you be clockin' dollars so I can get *mine. And* my sister. Or we gon' be all over you like a rash."

Aisha promised that if she made it, she'd "do the right thing" by Keeba, Teesha, Toya—all her homegirls. They settled back into TV and snacks and time passed like sleep.

Louis Sr.'s height genes had skipped a generation, making for a statuesque Ebony and a tall-for-her-age Starlett. What Aisha got were her mother's dense bones, which formed a squat frame for her fleshy body. Growing up alone with a distant mother, Aisha discovered that not only did food taste good, eating itself was soothing. Feeding herself became an act of love. The slow smear of thick brown peanut butter across a soft square of white bread, the swath of mayonnaise, the buttery cheese toast, hot and dripping—these were rituals in a small world of pleasure controlled absolutely by her.

When she had money, there were red hots, jawbreakers, SweeTarts, Chuckles, and chocolate kisses. Salted treats made her mouth squirt—potato chips and curled cheese puffs, vinegar-flavored potato sticks, and ridgy corn chips.

A little more money bought real food like hamburgers and hot dogs, fries and onion rings, pizza and hero sandwiches, all washed down in floods of sugary cherry, orange, grape, or cola-colored drinks. As Aisha's cooking skills grew, so did the stacks of pancakes, mounds of mashed potatoes, and piles of fried chicken parts.

Swathed in blankets and supported by pillows, Aisha would sink onto her bed with a tray full of food on her lap, absently engaged in one after another cartoon, soap opera, sitcom. As she developed outward but not upward, her breasts ballooned, her hips spread, and her thighs thickened. Constant eating became a way of life, something that happened almost automatically, like breathing.

In the projects, Aisha's size wasn't unusual, nor was it criticized, as most girls her age were large. With her dark eyes, strong cheekbones, and full, sensuous lips, Aisha was one of the prettiest girls around. So why *couldn't* she be a rich and famous big model?

Aisha could hear phones ringing nonstop in the background as the 1-800-BIGMODELS operator rattled off questions about Aisha's eye and hair color, height and weight, and gave her an address in lower Manhattan. "Take the elevator to the second floor, hang a right, go three doors down, then hang a left, and BIGMODELS is at the end of the corridor. Bring a headshot and your book, if you have one. If not, on-site makeup people and photographers will set up a shoot for you in the offices." Aisha wanted to do a dance. The operator added that there was an "absolutely nonrefundable fifty-dollar appointment and processing fee." She asked Aisha three times if Aisha understood that the agency was "only a conduit" and that "go-sees" were each girl's responsibility. "BIGMODELS gets twenty-five percent of your catalog work and forty percent for runway work. Totally standard in the business."

Aisha's brain got stuck on the fifty-dollar fee, and she hadn't paid much attention to the rest. Where was she gonna get the money? The lady in the Spanish store cashed food stamps but charged double what it cost to cash a real check. Whatever. If that's what it took to blow up and get paid . . . Puffy probably had to put up cash in the beginning to make his CDs. And Tyra must've had to dish out the benjamins to *her* first model agency too. Aisha saw this as her one chance and wasn't nothing stopping her. She was a fox, built like a brick house, and could model, dance in videos, do movies, whatever the agency wanted.

Ten

The morning of her appointment, Aisha admired herself in the mirror. She'd greased down her bang and swooped it to the side. Sporting her special fake gold trunk earrings, she felt good about her appearance. She was about to find out what the outside world felt about it.

The receptionist looked from the "don't make me kick ya ass" expression on Aisha's face to the Polaroids in her hand and back at Aisha's face. The morning was *not* going to be good.

"You got an appointment?" the young woman asked Aisha, an "I doubt it" tone in her voice. Her eyes examined Aisha's swirled bang, traced down to her jumbo maroon jacket, lingered at the too-tight blouse, fixed on the black leggings, and stopped in horror at the wide, run-down pumps. Aisha gave her name and admired the pictures of models on the walls while the receptionist turned pages in a thick calendar book.

"Ingram . . . Ingram . . . well, well, you're definitely in here. You got photos and the fee?"

She did. Her attention was directed to a pile of forms. "Fill out one of those. A rep will be with you shortly. I'll take the money now, thank you." Aisha squeezed her hand into the small coin pocket of her leggings and wiggled out a ball of crumpled bills.

"Cash? You don't have a check or money order?"

Aisha raised her eyebrows. This snotty babe was beginning to bug her.

"Do it *look* like I got a check or money order? You see cash, don't you?"

The receptionist primped her lips like she was about to say something real stank. Instead, she swallowed and said in a flat voice, "Cash will do fine. And I'll take your—er—snapshots too."

Aisha didn't like the way she flipped through the Polaroids Toya had taken, like they weren't good enough, and she *really* didn't like how she stuck them in a folder and wrote on it "Ingram, Asha."

" 'Scuse me, my name got a *i* in it."

"What?"

"I said you ain't spelled my name right. It got a *i*."

"The *i*'s right there," snapped the woman, pointing. "I-n-g-r-a-m. That *is* how you spell *Ingram*, I assume."

"I ain't talkin' about my last name." Dammit, Toya had

said a million times "Don't say *ain't*," and this wench had already made her mess up. "I mean *Aisha*, A-i-s-h-a."

The receptionist exhaled hard, snatched up a pen, and scrawled an *i* between the *A* and *s*. "Does *that* work for you?"

"Yes, it *do*." Aisha sat down as a smiling, heavyset woman wearing a dark pantsuit and a flip of thick, bouncy hair appeared at the reception desk with a very pretty, shapely girl to whom she was saying, "I think we just might be able to make it happen, Holly." She said to the receptionist, "Pammie, schedule Holly for a shoot early next week. I have her deposit."

Debbie Silver, president and executive director of BIG-MODELS, Incorporated, glanced at Aisha, then tried to catch Pammie's eye. But the receptionist and Holly were bent over the appointment calendar smiling and chatting. Miss Silver, a former professional model whose weight problems had forced her to stop modeling, asked Aisha, "Have you been helped?"

Aisha, nervous and excited, blurted out, "Oh, snap, you the one from the commercial! Phat!" When she stood, she didn't even reach Miss Silver's shoulder.

Miss Silver's feeling about this girl went from disapproval to dislike. Loud and unpolished. She cut a look at Pammie, who had finished with Holly and was watching the scene.

Pammie read her boss's face and reacted. "Debbie, this is Asha—A-*eye*-sha, excuse me—Ingram—"

"It's A-*eee*-sha," corrected Aisha, "*eee* like *pee*."

73

The receptionist ignored Aisha and continued, "—who saw our commercial and wants to model." She averted her eyes and flipped pages of a magazine, barely smothering the giggle building in her throat. These girls were too much, she thought, thinking they could traipse in there and become big models just because they were fat, as if that were enough. This one had a pretty face, but the hair, the clothes, those beat-up shoes—plus she was a midget by model standards. And "*eee* like *pee*"? How rude! She flipped more pages.

Debbie Silver straightened her back, asked for "Miss Aisha Ingram's folder," and told Aisha to follow her. Aisha took in the president's office while Miss Silver skimmed the application and waiver form and scrutinized the Polaroids.

The walls were plastered with black-and-white headshots and full-length color photos, some autographed, of glamorous women dressed in luxurious clothing. On the desk, turned so that both she and her clients had a full view, was a gold-framed photograph of a younger Debbie Silver, skeletal in a tight, fuchsia sequined gown. The shot had been taken at the height of her career and had run in all the major magazines.

Aisha heard Keeba's voice in her head: *"Go on in there and git yours! Don't lay back."* She smoothed down her bang and went for hers. "So Miss Silver, people say I'm nice-looking, and you can see I'm big, so that's why I'm here, to be a big model and get some money to take care of my family. I could model oversize jeans or do food commercials or be a thong girl in a music video . . ."

The BIGMODELS founder held in a smile. The kid was clueless—charming in a street sort of way, but definitely clueless. Not exactly representative of the audience their clients were trying to reach. A Brooklyn native herself, Debbie Silver had grown up in a neighborhood that changed during her teenage years from Jewish middle class to black and underclass. She recognized Aisha's look: project girl. She watched Aisha, saying nothing. Not much fashion potential. But the kid had gotten the fee together, God knew how, and had come in to try her luck. That showed heart—a trait she respected.

"Tell me about your background, Miss Ingram—schooling, work experience. You said you're supporting a family?"

Aisha's eyes brightened. "Yeah, I got two kids, Starlett Whitney who just turned four—"

"Don't tell me, she's named for Whitney Houston, correct?"

"Yeah, how'd you know?! What, you one of them 1-800 fortune-tellers too?"

"No, no, far from it. I'd have won Lotto by now. Just a feeling," said Debbie. It seemed like every day she was getting a call or a letter from a Whitney this or Whitney that. "Please, go on." She was beginning to like the kid.

"And the other one's Ty, who's two. All right, Miss 1-800, who *he* named after?"

Debbie laughed. "I have absolutely no idea, but to humor you, I'll hazard a wild guess—Mike Tyson?"

"Ugh, no! Not *him*. Ty-*rese*. The singer. Now *he* love women, he don't beat on them, and he fine too. So I'm staying with my moms for the moment until I find . . ."

Aisha's voice trailed off as the worry over welfare filled her again. Miss Silver's eyes on her gave her a sad feeling, but she chased it away. "As for school, I probably be going back."

"To college?"

"High school. To finish up. Gotta take a couple more classes."

"Umm-hmm." A high school dropout with little children and still living at home, thought Debbie. That's a tough one. The girl has guts, coming in with nothing going for her but hope. Still, she wasn't running a charity. Few of her clients would be interested in . . . Better tell the kid up front, refund her money. It was only fair.

"I'll be honest with you, Miss—"

"Can I just say something, Miss Silver? You look a hundred times better now than on that picture!" interrupted Aisha, pointing to the picture frame. "When I first looked at it, I was like, 'Damn, Miss Silver need a big plate of macaroni and cheese, barbecue ribs, and collard greens.' I'd buy a outfit I saw on *you* before I'd want anything swinging off *her* bones."

Debbie Silver listened, this time not hiding her smile. Scores of aspiring and actual models had sat in that same chair and enthused about her "gorgeous" photo. She played along, when in truth it was there to remind her—and them—of how unhealthy it all was, the not eating, the throwing up, the mad quest to look skinny. A young woman's body was not intended to look like a twelve-year-old's. A simple fact of nature.

She examined Aisha again, the slicked hair, chipped bangle earrings, and bursting blouse. Her style was hopeless, but she was a natural beauty. There might be *something*. It would be a very long shot, but hell, it might pay off—for them both.

Aisha could've smacked herself. Everything was going good until she ragged on the picture. Why she always had to talk out her neck, say things that got on people's last nerve? She rubbed her nose and did a fake cough. "Umm . . . I hope you not . . . I wasn't trying to . . ."

Debbie shrugged. "No problem, Aisha, I appreciate honesty. I can call you by your first name?"

"Uh-huh," nodded Aisha, "everybody do. *Debbie*."

"*Debbie* can work. You're right. I was one of the walking dead at that shoot and for much of my short career, and you're one of the few to call it as she sees it. In return, I'm going to be honest with you. Your look is not what our institutional clients typically require in models of *any* size. Your hair, your clothes, your height, your weight—all wrong. But you're a beauty."

Aisha said, "Whatever." Debbie smiled.

"Oh yes, and the attitude. Wrong. But I said *typically.*

We also work niche markets for smaller companies. They wouldn't use you to sell snacks to teens in Casper, Wyoming. They'd get a five-foot-eight blond, outdoorsy type. You'd be tapped by the client targeting a hipper, more urban audience. Madison Avenue knows that beauty depends on community. The toothpick look they've sold so well to white girls has less appeal among ethnic whites and no appeal to blacks, where attractive means 'baby got back.' "

"Ahhh—ha, ha—" sputtered Aisha, gasping. "You *too* funny! I mean . . . how somebody white know about *back*!"

"It's part of my job to know trends in clothes, hair, and even expressions. And when you live with a sixteen-year-old who blasts Sir Mix-A-Lot as soon as she gets into the house, you learn more than you ever wanted to know about the beauty of big butts."

Aisha was fascinated. She was in a fancy office in Manhattan talking with a white lady about rap and big butts. What a trip! The conversation switched to business matters such as fine-tuning Aisha's look, what goes on at go-see interviews and photo shoots, and pay scales for television, catalog, and runway work. Aisha knew better than to let herself get all juiced, but all sorts of fantasies were spinning in her head.

The two of them walked out of the president's office like buddies.

"Pammie, Aisha's going to need a fresh book—you'll find a couple of extras in the cabinet behind you—and she needs new photos." She gave Aisha a playful nudge. "Polaroids might've been good enough for Warhol but not for *real* girls."

Aisha had no idea who or what she was talking about, so she just said, "Word."

"Squeeze her in with Sam for sometime after lunch, say about two."

"But Miss Silver, she only paid for—"

"It's fine. Oh yes, I have a two-thirty with Gap and a four o'clock with the Ann Taylor people, which'll probably go late, so I won't be back in today. And Pammie, refund Aisha's fee. This one's on me."

"But Miss Silver, the policy says—"

"*I* made the policy, and in this instance *I'm* changing it." Debbie Silver grabbed Aisha's hand. "It's been a pleasure. I'll be in touch if I can shake anything loose."

"Thank you, Debbie." Aisha grinned.

"Debbie?" mumbled the receptionist under her breath.

eleven

The noontime streets swarmed with people buying food, eating food, carrying food in bags. As "all wrong" as Miss Silver had said she was, Aisha felt very right at that moment bumping her way through the throngs. Matter of fact, she felt fly. Supa dupa fly, as Aisha's favorite hip-hop star Missy Elliott would say. She coulda swore that every boy's eye she caught had a special glint in it, and that all the girls she outstared looked jealous.

Aisha swayed and sashayed her hips as she approached the hot dog stand. "Lemme get two franks with everything, a pretzel with extra mustard, and a root beer—" A thought cut short her sentence. "No, make that a *diet* root beer." Better shed a few pounds. But not too many, 'cause Miss Silver was dead right about girls needing meat on they bones.

She squeezed onto the end of a crowded bench in City Hall Park and balanced the cardboard tray on her knees. Soon she was washing down the last of her lunch with big gulps of soda. Workers returned to their jobs, and Aisha slid to the middle of the bench into a warm shaft of sunlight. The fantasies returned. *I'ma be a model. I'ma be a model.* She burped and loosened the drawstring on her leggings.

A parade of cars curled onto the Brooklyn Bridge. On the other side of the river were the projects, where she was born. She squinted at the tall, uniform buildings so far off. No, there would be no workfare for Aisha Ingram. No scrub brushes and dirty water, no heavy brooms or pointy trash pickup poles, and definitely no getting her butt kicked hassling folks on no subway patrol. She was about to blow up. No bout a-doubt it. *Big.* Big respect, big shoutouts, and big benjamins was all coming her way. Across the street, shoppers flowed in and out of the revolving doors of J & R Music World. If she had the cash, she'd be in there too, buying Whitney's greatest and Brandy's latest and Janet's newest. Well, she *did* have her fifty dollars. The double clang of a church chime jolted her. Sam! He *betta* be cute. Across the park she ran, bouncing and jiggling, and bustled down Broadway.

Mornings at the agency were usually calm, the appointments for intakes and interviews carefully spaced. Afternoons were tumultuous, with girls waiting to be photographed, primping for go-sees, returning from shoots, and excitedly trading tales.

"Omigod, she was like, 'Stacey, you are sooo going on the Waikiki shoot'—I almost fainted . . ."

". . . so I says to him, 'Excuuuuse-me, this *was* a call for big models—am I right or am I wrong?—and now you telling me I gotta lose ten pounds? I don't *think* so.' "

"Swear to God on a mountain of Bibles, Viv, he walked in the studio wearing nothing but his cameras, and he had all this gross, red hair—ugh, it was disgusting . . ."

"I'm okay. I guess. But that was my *eleventh* go-see. Girls are getting work their *first* time out, but people look at me like 'Vanish from my world!' One of these days I'm going to just stick my naked behind in an art director's face and scream, 'Here's where you can put your go-see. Go to hell! See?' "

The boasting, complaining, and moaning were in full blast when the door banged open and in lunged Aisha, instantly silencing all talk. Sweat beaded her brow and darkened the armpits of her blouse, which had finally popped open under the strain. Her carefully smashed-down bang had been blown upward from her run and was sticking out like the brim of a cap.

"Where Sam at?!" she panted. Whispers rose.

Pammie's face registered the disdain she hadn't dared show in front of her boss. She pulled out Aisha's file, looked inside, then dropped it on the desk.

"You were scheduled for two o'clock, not ten after. Sam is very busy and cannot be kept waiting. I already sent another girl. Have a seat. Modeling is *so* about punctually keeping appointments."

A few girls nodded in agreement. A project girl dissed is a force of nature. A plume of heat climbed Aisha's spine, fanned through her back, gathered in her neck, and spread to her ears and face. Her eyes sparked, and a tremor shot through her body that seemed to be felt by the whole group. "Uh-oh," whispered a voice. As though their sky had grown suddenly dark, the models filled the office with anxious murmurs and edgy movements like forest animals sensing danger.

"No, you *didn't* give away my appointment that was for *about* two o'clock, or I'ma be *so* about punctually kicking your stank butt!" A couple of girls eased out the door.

Pammie, a proud Long Islander, was not about to take that from Brooklyn trash. She said out loud to no one in particular, "These ghetto girls are so mouthy, it's not even funny! They get their fee refunded and a free book for their photos, then they have the gall to come in late for a shoot they haven't even paid for! I swear, some people are always looking for a freebie like somebody *owes* them. This isn't the frigging welfare, it's a model agency."

She got up from her desk. "Look, *honey*, you're *late*. So take a seat and wait your turn like everybody else. Nobody gets special treatment around here."

Aisha walked slowly around the desk and stood nose to

bosom with the tall, athletic receptionist. Not a girl remained in the room. In the hallway, urgent voices called, "Sam! Sam!"

"What you mean by *ghetto* girls? Why you gotta go *there* when you know ya *mama's* the one who be ghetto! What, you wanna piece of me?" challenged Aisha, ready to fight.

Their bodies pressed hard on one another as if each were trying to walk right through the other.

Aisha was defiant despite being outmatched physically. "And I ain'tcha honey! Do I *look* like some white girl's honey?! Now back up off me!" She pushed forward, attitude made flesh. "Back up *off* me, I said."

"*You* back up, homegirl, all the way outta here, before I call the cops!" Pammie planted herself firmly against Aisha, a solid mass of former college basketball star.

"*Call* 'em, g'head! My *sister* a cop! And you wrong about nobody gettin' special treatment 'cause you 'bout to get treated right now!"

Aisha gave the receptionist a hard shove, throwing her backward against the wall. Pammie gripped Aisha's forehead like she was palming a basketball and held her at arm's length. Aisha swung wildly with serious determination, but her arms were just too short to land a single punch.

That didn't stop her though from shouting as if she were really beating Pammie down. "Yeah, uh-huh, how ya like me now?! I *told* you to back up, but you had to be *all that*."

Pammie's large hand was gripping Aisha's whole face, but the lips kept moving. "That's all you got?! You ain't nothin'. *Now* who's all that, Miss Telephone Girl?! Who's all that now?!"

Pammie glared. "It sure isn't you, chubby. Just what are you supposed to be doing? *You're* the one who's nothing!"

Using her upper-body strength and still holding Aisha by the face, she pushed her toward the door. Aisha spun around, breaking Pammie's grip, ducked, and lunged. Both girls went crashing to the floor, Aisha banging away at Pammie's brick-hard abdominals as though she were pounding her way out of a life closing in on her. All of a sudden forceful hands grabbed Aisha under the armpits and yanked her backward.

"What in the name of—are you *crazy*?! Get *off* her! Somebody get a cop up here!" Samantha was a powerfully built woman with a river of silky black hair and a gifted eye for photography. She'd been shooting Debbie Silver's big models for a year. But this was a first! Sam pulled Aisha off the receptionist, who was panting more from surprise than anything else.

"You okay, Pammie?! What's going on in here?!"

The models had returned and were huddled in the doorway.

"Stacey, help me get her inside to Debbie's couch. Viv, bring wet paper towels from the ladies' room!"

Pammie leaped to her feet. "I'm fine, Sam, really! That

wuss can't even punch." She moved toward Aisha. "You didn't hurt me, dough girl, you're too soft to hurt anything. That's why you got your fat face palmed! Try me again, and I'll dunk you!"

"Oh, you gon' *dunk* me?! Step to me then, donkey, step to me!"

Sam jumped between the fighters and held them apart. "Someone please call 911! Now!"

Aisha snatched her file from the desk and ran as fast as she could.

Twelve

The Brooklyn Bridge—its cooling air, project views, and
solid walkway—calmed her as it carried her back home.
The timepiece on the famous Clock Building said three
o'clock. She remembered how that had been her favorite
time of day, when school was about to let out and freedom
was so close she felt it in her body. Her legs would get to
jumping as if the double-dutch rope were already flying,
holding her in its magical whirl. Raven would get the three
o'clock bug too, and soon their teacher'd be hollering,
"Aisha! Raven! Sit still." Or Aisha would jerk back and forth
in her seat, ducking in her imagination the dodgeball always aimed at her legs. At those times, the teacher'd give
her a girls' room pass without even asking if she had to go.
Once in the hall, she'd tear through school, drumming on
classroom doors, and leaping down steps three at a time.

It was true, thought Aisha, that she busted out a lot of energy, but she never wanted nothing much more than to have fun. If anyone had told her then where she'd be at nineteen, she wouldn'ta believed it. She had really wanted to lock down a modeling job, but she screwed it up. Why hadn't she just dealt with it like *whatever* and acted cool? She coulda met the girls, maybe made friends, got her book together. Why'd she always have to get in a fight like a hoodlum? Pammie had dissed her in front of everybody, but so what? Had she put her hands on her? No. And s'pose the cops had busted her and locked her up? What about Star and Ty?

Aisha arrived at the bottom of the walkway steps, still blaming herself for the abrupt end of her modeling dream. She lifted the top off a trash can and tossed in her BIG-MODELS file.

"Mommy!" cheered Starlett, hearing her mother's voice in the doorway.

Teesha could tell from Aisha's face not to bug her about how long it took her to come pick up her kids.

Aisha gave Starlett a tight hug and swung her in circles, gripping her small hands. "Been good?"

"Yeah, Mommy. And look what I drew for you! Me and you and Ty riding Black Fury the flying horsie I saw on TV!" Starlett waved her crayon-scrawled drawing.

"That's pretty." Aisha lifted Ty and balanced him on her

hip. "And how you been, bad little boy? You been a good bad little boy? He was okay, Teesha?"

"He was okay. Cried, ate, pooped. Baby stuff. Why your hair so messed up? Or did they send you to the East Village to model?"

Cradling her son, Aisha told Teesha the story, how Debbie Silver had liked her and refunded her money even though she wasn't s'pose to, how Aisha'd gotten on a diet at lunchtime, and how she blew it all by letting some snotty office wench bug her out. Teesha said the whole thing was wak from the get-go because they probably only wanted white girls.

"Nah, Teesha, it wasn't even about white and black. I know Miss Silver woulda tried to hook me up—she was mad cool. But now after I done whipped her office girl's behind . . . well, would *you* be hot to gimme a job?"

"Nope. I'd be waiting at the door with a bat in case the maniac came back! Nah, but on the serious tip, you think they gon' send the cops after you?"

"They can't. They don't know nothin' about me, 'cause I grabbed my file when I ran. What make me so mad is that Miss Silver was gonna give me a chance even though I wasn't the right type of model, and I had to go and break wild."

"Ai, you know what me and my sister been saying for years—that you gotta chill on the girl thug thing. You been beefin' with folks long as I know you, and that's long. All of us is pissed off at *some*body, but you got *kids* now. Your Tupac days is over. Just like his is."

"You right, I know. Whatever. Hey, you got anything to eat? A plump spongy Sno Ball would definitely hit the spot."

"Like hungry children, like hungry mama! What y'all Ingrams think this is, the day care *and* the welfare? All we got is canned sardines."

"Nasty! I hope you ain't fed that cat food to my kids!"

Teesha laughed out loud. "I couldn't get them kitties to *stop* eating."

"Gimme some sardines then. I'll eat anything right now. But pick out the bones first."

"Keep dreamin'. Just 'cause you whipped Pammie Whitegirl's butt don't think you gon' be bossing me around, 'cause you playin' yaself in front of ya kittens."

She pushed Aisha down onto the couch. Aisha stayed put, too worn out to do much more. They ate sardines on crackers and listened to Anastacia. It was agreed that she *had* to be black with a phat voice like that, no matter *how* blond she was. After a while, Aisha collected her family and went home. Louise was waiting for her.

"Here. Your mail. I don't want to know nothin' about it. I wash my hands. But I tell you this, come rent time, I'll be expecting your part. With God as my witness, I can't carry myself, another grown woman, and two hungry, growing children on my measly check."

Aisha hurried to her room with the letter.

Dear Ms. Ingram,

Your time limits for cash assistance will be expiring as indicated in this notice. Our records as of the date hereof contain no response from you to the Department's 60-Day or 30-Day Notices regarding the 5-year lifetime limit on aid which you will have reached ten (10) business days from the date of this Final Termination Notice. Further, we have no record of your enrollment in our Strict Caring Readjustment Effort to Work to End Dependency program popularly known as "Workfare," which provides recipients a transition stipend under specified conditions. YOUR PUBLIC ASSISTANCE BENEFITS SHALL TERMINATE ON THE DATE INDICATED BELOW. YOU MUST CONTACT THIS OFFICE WITHIN THE NEXT TEN (10) BUSINESS DAYS IF YOU WISH TO ENROLL IN WORKFARE. *The Department of Public Assistance encourages you, Aisha Ingram, to take full advantage of this exciting opportunity. To that end, we hope you will schedule an appointment with the undersigned caseworker to discuss how you plan to manage your household expenses.*

Yours sincerely,
Charles Covington Poncie III

Louise had shuffled back to her bedroom, her slippers scratching on the floor like sandpaper. Aisha knew what time it was—time to deal. Finished were the days of fantasies and dreams and ideas that ended where they began—in her head. Nope, wasn't no surprises behind doors or lucky breaks around the bend for a project girl on welfare with no schooling, two kids, and a mother with extra clean hands. Tomorrow morning she'd go see her caseworker.

Thirteen

To Aisha's surprise, her mother agreed, without complaining, to watch the kids while Aisha went to the welfare department. She wanted to save on bus fare, so she walked the nine blocks. A drab building of gray brick rose twelve stories above the street. A sudden shower was falling. Aisha tried to shield her hot-combed hair under a newspaper, but it was no use. The smooth bang that had lain so close to her head was puffy, and the hair she'd slicked down tight on the sides was thick.

The main office, patrolled by a trio of armed security guards, consisted of cubicles the caseworkers proudly called their "areas." In and out of the small boxes came the welfare clients, some looking worried, others angry, still others just defeated. No one looked happy. The place had a sharp, closed smell like some living thing had settled in its vents long ago and died there.

Chuck Poncie, disenchanted lawyer turned social worker, waved to Aisha from his cubicle. "Well, well—a visit from my favorite client. I was beginning to think you were, what do you kids say, *igging* my letters. Those who do, do so at their peril. The department giveth and the department taketh away. Please," he said, pointing to a metal chair, "have a seat and tell me your heart's desire. Shall it be door number one's graffiti busters, door number two's clean sweepers, or door number three's subway patrol?"

Why he always had to be wak, she did *not* know, but today was *not* the day to be acting cute. She plopped down, crossing her arms on her stomach. "I don't want *no* door. I'm here under distress."

"I believe you mean *duress*."

"I know what kinda stress I mean. I got a heart condition, Mr. Poncie. I can't *be* out there washing walls and sweeping streets."

Mr. Poncie pulled a page from her file. "Hmmm, no mention *here* of health problems. C'mon Aisha, the government—and I—would like to see you live a self-sufficient, independent life. Back when I was in juvenile defense, I thought keeping youngsters out of lockup would save them. But what you kids truly need, I realized, is a mechanism that prepares you for entry-level jobs."

Aisha picked at the cuticle of her thumb and exhaled hard, as if her last breath had left her.

"For heaven's sake, don't look so grim. Workfare never killed anybody. That is, that I know of." She looked on with no expression as her caseworker laughed, slapping his thigh.

"Yeah, you g'head and crack yaself up, Mr. Poncie. But you gon' be crying and hollering at my casket after my heart give out."

That remark got him going so loud that the caseworker in the next cubicle asked, "Who's in with *you*, Poncie, funnyman Chris Tucker?"

"My lord," he said, wiping his eyes, "you're a piece of work, Aisha. It's a shame there's no workfare comedy troupe, because you'd be perfect! Okay, can we get down to business here? I need your choice."

Aisha had decided when the first notice came that, if forced into workfare, she'd choose whatever was least embarrassing and wouldn't make her sweat her clothes. That left only one choice.

"The subway thing."

"Excellent selection! Can I be honest with you? That's where I see you best utilizing your skills."

"Skills? What skills? A monkey can yoke and choke roughnecks jumping turnstiles and robbing people."

"That may be. Monkeys are indeed capable of performing many learned tasks, and I'm impressed that you would know that. But you're no monkey, and your job won't be to *yoke* anyone. We have police for that. Let me tell you a little about our patrollers. They may deal directly only with those committing minor infractions—smoking, drinking, blasting music, spitting, skating, and the like. The youth patrols operate in a non–law enforcement fashion, not unlike the Guardian Angels. Are you familiar with them?"

"*Puh-leeze.* Nobody scared of them Urkels in red tams. They punks."

Mr. Poncie frowned. "*They're* punks? You teens, you're all so tough. Well, you'd be surprised how many tough guys—and gals—who call themselves 'thugs for life' and the rest of that nonsense boo-hoo like babies when they find themselves locked up."

"Then *they* punks too. Don't do the crime if you can't do the time, that's what I say." Aisha knew he hated when she acted all ghetto-down and was glad to be having an effect on him, pissing him off.

"Oh, is *that* what you say, Miss Ingram? Do you want to know what *I* say?"

"Nope." She stretched in her chair, yawned, and refolded her arms across her stomach.

"I say *that* attitude, and I see it in here every single day—cavalier, street, supposedly hip—shows a tragic indifference to your own future and to that of—"

"Yada, yada, yada." She had the upper hand and was glad to wield it. He could take away her money, but at least she could get on his last nerve.

"Excuse me? What did you say?" She watched his jaw jump.

"I *said*, Mr. Poncie, ya—da—ya—da—ya—da." And she flashed a broad grin.

"Fine," he said coldly. Mumbling to himself, he went on,

"I swear to God, you try to help these brats—fine. Yada *this*." He handed her a large envelope marked *Subway Youth Patrol Info Packet*. "Report next Monday at eight to the Grand Central Station supervisor for orientation. Be late, by even one minute, and your case is closed for noncooperation. Have a nice day, Miss Ingram."

"I always do."

Aisha made sure Poncie heard her humming as she left his area. Once outside she inhaled deeply and pushed from her chest the welfare's dead breath. The rain had stopped, and the drying sidewalks and streets glistened. A tree dropped a splat of water onto her head. What would she have to do as a patrol girl? Was it dangerous? Scary? Fun? Didn't much matter anymore really. "A girl gotta do what a girl gotta do," she said aloud, heading home.

She eased into the apartment, dreading the angry questions and snide comments that were sure to greet her. The sight she saw stopped her smack in the doorway. Louise had decorated all their faces with powder, lips with lipstick, and eyes with eyeliner. In her usual housewear, she was stepping in rhythm to a recording of the Miss America theme song she had from years back. Starlett, draped in a sheet, holding her head high, paraded behind, and Ty stumbled in circles, beaming with newly blackened eyebrows.

"What is y'all . . . ?" She scratched her head. "Well, I guess that's it—the whole family done bugged *out*. Y'all hav-

ing a Halloween party, and October ain't even here yet."
Keeping an eye on the kids was one thing, but since when
did Louise *play* with them?

Louise lowered the music and eyed her daughter's head.
"Umm-hmm, and I see *you* ready for Halloween too with
your afro. Where your dashiki?" Her own humor tickled
her no end.

The sight of their grandmother doubled over made the
kids laugh. Aisha glimpsed herself in the hall mirror and
couldn't help but join in. She loved those rare moments
that caught Louise in a good mood, the anger eased, the
drinking on hold. And seeing her mother in makeup,
Aisha saw the ghost of the teen beauty queen Lil' Lou had
been. It was sad—dreams and Ingrams just didn't seem to
go together.

"You so crazy, Ma. Make fun if you want to. But I better
not catch any of y'all sneaking in the subway when I'm on
patrol, or it's gon' be ugly." She slid onto the floor between
the children.

Louise sat down too, tucking her housecoat under her.
"If that's what them workfare folk got you doing, it's fine by
me, but not that other mess. Any wall you wash or floor you
sweep better be in this apartment. Ingrams wasn't made to
be no outdoor maids."

"Who told you? How'd you know about . . . ?" Now Aisha
was the one bugging. She hadn't said anything about workfare. Plus, Louise was so out of it most of the time, how'd
she . . .

"Oh child, please, a mother knows. When you been one as long as I been, you'll know things too. A mother knows, that's all."

Their eyes met and lingered, but neither woman found words to say. Ty rubbed his hands red with a tube of lipstick he found at the foot of the couch. Starlett leaned into her mommy's shoulder, smearing mocha blush on Aisha's sleeve. Louise hummed along with the man singing "Here she comes, Miss America!" a faint smile on her red lips. There on the floor, surrounded by family, Aisha felt it was all good.

After dinner, Aisha washed dishes, turned on her favorite radio show, Hot FM's *BlackLikeDat Old School Grooves*, and opened the envelope Poncie gave her. The folder inside was stamped "Metropolitan Transit Authority New York City." A pamphlet about "Old New York" had a black-and-white cover picture of women in long dresses and men in suits and hats. "The Dutch bought Manhattan from the Native Americans for $24 worth of trinkets," she read. *Boy, that ain't right—them Indians got played.* "New York was briefly the U.S. capital from 1789 to 1790." She smiled with pride. *We always been da bomb, and ya know dat! Ran the whole country before Chocolate City took over.*

Humming to Rose Royce's "Wishing on a Star," she flipped through the info sheets, stopping at "The Busters Buff It Up—New York's Graffiti Removal Program." Glaring at her from a color picture were two teenage girls, four women who looked her mother's age, and a young man, all in matching blue MTA BUSTERS T-shirts and work gloves. Wearing tight smiles, they stood shoulder to shoulder holding spray cans and blocky sponges. Aisha made a face. *Look at them poor scrubs. You can tell from they faces they ain't really down with it. Half of them look like they the ones be bombing whole cars and throwing up they own wild style tags on walls.*

She opened the pamphlet: a picture of a man with a squarish head and a woman with pinched lips and a tiny bow tie. "Graffiti is not art. It is a blight. Today, thanks to the work of BUFF, our graffiti removal program, the once-notorious defacements of so-called graffiti 'artists' have been wiped from the face of our City by an enthusiastic team of volunteers from the Department of Public Assistance. MTA Executive Director S. K. Marks joins Transit Authority President Lana Retenza in saluting these New Yorkers."

Louise called from her bedroom. The kids had fallen asleep watching *Martin*. Aisha put down her papers, stretched, and went to her mother's room. She was propped against about a hundred pillows, and Star was crossways at the end of the bed. Ty lay perpendicular to his sister, his foot on the back of her head.

"You awfully quiet in there."

Aisha told her what she was reading. "Did you know, Ma, that white people bought Manhattan from the Indians for some fake jewelry like they be selling in the mall?"

"Girl, everything white folks *got* came from lying, stealing, or tricking somebody. How many years they had us slaving for free, now they gon' kick poor folk off welfare saying we the freeloaders. Please."

"I hear that." She hesitated. "Ma, I know your check ain't enough to—well, that me and the kids gonna have to—I just want you to know that I tried to keep my checks, but nothing worked out."

Louise closed her eyes. Long ago she had tried to substitute the dream of a perfect family for her own failed dreams of glamour and fortune, but without success. As time passed, her children had grown up, and she and her husband had grown apart. Louis worked constantly, and when he wasn't working, he hung out in jazz clubs with his buddies. Oftentimes he had come home late and sometimes not at all. First the happiness of marriage, then the joys of motherhood fizzled. The twins moved, Ebony fled. Before her stood her last child, Aisha. Louise opened her eyes and whispered, "Good night, baby," to her daughter.

Aisha lifted Ty and shook Starlett. "Come on, Star, come get in bed." Once they were tucked in, she lowered the volume on the radio and, bouncing to Marvin Gaye's "What's Goin' On," resumed reading. She opened "Subway Facts and Figures." "The New York City Subway system officially opened in 1904 with 28 subway stations. Today, it is the most extensive public transportation system in the world, running 24 hours and serving 468 stations and 4.3 million riders a day." *Yeah, they got that right,* smirked Aisha, *and all four million of them homeys be squeezing into the A train any time I be trying to get on.*

"Damn!" she exclaimed, reading that 36.2 million riders a year passed through Grand Central Terminal, the same station she had to go to for orientation. She was not looking forward to fitty million people getting in her face. Why couldn't they keep her in Brooklyn? Poncie probably sent her there on purpose to get her back for yada-yada-yada.

The oldies hour was coming to an end. Aisha bounced in bed to Chaka Khan singing "I'm Every Woman." The last info sheet she read was the only one she was really interested in: "Subway Youth Patrol (SYP)—Don't Just Say No, Say Zero." No photo. Good. She did *not* want her face in no picture with a group of fake DTs. All her friends *hated* them undercover detectives in the subway. You do one little thing, and they bust you. Some of them be disguised like bums and bag ladies. Probably half the nuns riding them trains were packing steel in little ankle holsters under they smocks.

Frowning slightly when she began, Aisha's face was in a full grimace by the time she got to the end of the page. "The Mayor's Zero Tolerance Program has succeeded in reducing crime throughout the City. Offender profiles show that crime can start with a minor infraction. A mugger doesn't buy a token—he jumps the turnstile. A pickpocket shadowing a victim doesn't bother to find a trash can for her gum wrapper—she litters. Rowdy sports fans don't drink in taverns or at home as the law requires—they toast in public. These are situations where courageous Department of Public Assistance volunteers step in. Subway Youth Patrol volunteers stop in their tracks the token cheat, the litterer, and the public drinker. Serious infractions are signaled to a supervisor who radios on-duty police officers. SYP stops the rulebreaker, NYPD catches the lawbreaker— New York teamwork at its best! MTA Executive Director S. K. Marks joins Transit Authority President Lana Retenza in saluting these New Yorkers."

Though no one was around to see, she rolled her eyes and even made them flutter in disgust. That was the dumbest thing she ever heard. What if you *wasn't* a mugger, pickpocket, or rowdy? Busting people for dropping a wrapper or drinking a beer was stupid when the city was full of gangsters and killers. They could f'git it if they thought she was gonna drop a dime on people for stuff that wasn't even bad. No way. She collected her papers, stuck them back in the envelope, curled around Starlett, and fell asleep.

fourteen

Aisha hurried along the subway platform toward the group gathered outside the office next to the Grand Central Station token booth. In her head she heard Poncie's voice: *"Be late—by even one minute—and your case is closed."* It *couldn't* be after eight already! She'd given herself plenty of time. But everybody else was already there. She noticed a wall clock inside the token booth. It was only seven-fifty! Those welfare people must've scared the mess out of all of them. Ten "courageous volunteers" were milling around, yawning and checking each other out. Fifty percent of them were girls and fifty percent boys, and they all seemed a hundred percent pissed.

"Nobody best not call me no damn 'volunteer,' because I was forced into this mess! With their two-cent stipend I gotta *pay* somebody to watch my kids. So what we s'pose to *live* on?"

"I hear *that*, sister. Look at me, I been on lockdown myself, with damn near my whole hood, all of us political prisoners. And they want me to throw a few *more* brothers in the jaws of the system? Homey don't *think* so." The one who said that, Aisha noted, had a shaved head, deep-set dark brown eyes, and a nice physique.

"Hey, it's betta than being the clean-up woman. We ain't really gotta do nothin'," said a skinny girl with bad skin, picking at a scab on her shoulder. "They just betta have some food for us in that office—shoot, I'm hungry."

"First punk homey so much as *look* at me funny, I'm gon' make him my son, and that's *word*. Don't need no cop, supervisor, nobody to do what *I'm* out here to do, boyee. I was in Nam, know what I'm sayin'?"

Aisha felt like she knew these strangers, from school, from home, from life. They were dropouts and young mothers and guys with criminal records, all poor and at the mercy of men with squarish heads and women in bow ties.

"Eight o'clock! Roll call!" The voice came from inside the office. There was mumbling and grumbling as the supervisor appeared with a pad and pen. Aisha was so stunned, she barely heard her name called.

"Ingram, Aisha," repeated Mrs. Vinker, inspecting the faces of the group as if she didn't know what her son's ex-girlfriend and the mother of his two children looked like.

"I'm right *here*! You *know* you recogni—" She stopped. Kevin's mail-stealing mother was the supervisor of her Subway Youth Patrol section?! God was surely trying to punish her.

Mrs. Vinker made no response and continued down her list. "Iola, Cousine!" "Jackson, Rena!" "Johnson, Victor!" "Leeson, Catherine!" "Payne, Max!"

"Here!" shouted some. Others simply grunted, "Uh-huh." A couple had more to say.

"Niecy Mercherson!"

"Damn right I'm Niecy Mercherson. I wanna know when we get off? I *cannot* afford to spend the whole damn day doing this undercover crap. Where you welfare people think we s'pose to come up with money for baby-sitters when you done took away every penny we got?!"

"Powell, Retha!"

"When breakfast? Don't make me go off up in here, and my stomach burnin' already!"

Once the last person had answered "Yeah, wassup," the supervisor re-called Niecy Mercherson and Retha Powell.

"You two are free to leave. Go back to your caseworkers and choose another option, because Transit"—and here she looked each person in the eyes, lingering an extra second on Aisha—"tolerates no lip, whining, or attitude. Now the rest of you follow me." Niecy and Retha shouted curses and threats at her back as Mrs. Vinker led the group inside the cramped office.

Her blue-tinted gray hair was in tight curls on top of her head and was held back on the sides by long bobby pins that could double as weapons if necessary. In her fifteen years selling tokens and MetroCards under the streets of New York City, she never had to stick the pins in anything other than her hair. But in the past few years, clerks were being followed to their work stations and held up or their booths set on fire to force them out. So she didn't hesitate when Transit offered her a job outside the cage.

She glanced at Aisha, who was whispering to Max Payne, the good-looking bald guy.

"Do you have a question, Ingram, or can we get started?"

"No questions. I was just checking out the poster over the desk that say the subways is safe. But what about the B train that derailed at DeKalb Avenue last year and all them people got hurt. That's all."

"Word *up*! Why the trains in *our* hoods always crashing, derailing, and stalling? Y'all remember the Queens-bound A that bounced in Harlem? I was *on* that sucker, know what I'm sayin'? Man, folks was flipping like *pancakes*. A week later, I'm on the number 3 in Brooklyn, and *that* train run off the tracks at President Street. So wassup widdat? The city be saying they backed up on the repairs they gotta make, but it ain't about backlog, it's about *blacklog*, and that's *word*."

"Or maybe it's just you, brother," said Max.

They all laughed.

"People, you've just wasted six minutes of your orientation. And for your information, last April the number 5 derailed uptown at Fifty-ninth Street during rush hour. Thousands of people, including whites, were stuck in a tunnel for *hours* until we got a second train to them. So don't get caught up in racial paranoia. Some things that happen to minorities in this city *are* troubling, but killer subway trains aren't it. Now, did you all read the SYP info sheet?"

"Yeahs" echoed in the office.

Were there questions?

The "nahs" followed.

Mrs. Vinker handed each patroller a walkie-talkie, a SUB-WAY YOUTH PATROL cap, and a list of "infractions" they could handle on their own and "misdemeanors and crimes" to be reported to her. "All right. Remember, you're not cops or undercover detectives or even security guards. You're the MTA's Guardian Angels, no more and no less." With her eyes, she demonstrated "subtle" versus "provocative" observation. She assigned pairs, and within minutes the new patrollers were fanning out along the subway platforms, connecting corridors, and open passageways of the world's busiest subway station, Grand Central Terminal, for their first practice run. More training sessions followed and finally the SUBWAY YOUTH PATROL was ready to roll.

fifteen

It was nine o'clock. The mad morning rush was in full swing. Under the high vault of the station's starry ceiling, the main concourse was a picture of chaos. Pushing and bumping past each other on the pink marble floor, train commuters snorted "Excuse me" in the same tone as they'd say "Drop dead." In business suits and warm-up suits, wingtip shoes and tennis shoes, horn-rimmed glasses and sunglasses, they dashed and squeezed and elbowed their way in and out of the cars, shouting over the roar of steel wheels on rails, "I *said* 'excuse me'!"

The team of Aisha Ingram and Max Payne slowly climbed the sweeping staircase at the west end of the concourse. Max leaned against the balustrade of the balcony, and Aisha plumped down on the top step.

"Why they gotta act like animals to get to they boring jobs? I swear, the first person foot that so much as *touch* me gon' go flying down these steps." She filled her mouth with potato chips. Breakfast.

Max swallowed orange juice from a small container. "A buck fifty for *this*? Man, *that's* the crime. We should start our patrol career by arresting the owner of that store for robbery."

"Hey, it's all good. I got him back. Stole these chips." She crammed another handful into her mouth and wiped her fingers on her jeans. "Check out them chandeliers! I wish I could steal one of them for my room. Remember that crazy movie *Sleeping with the*—no, that wasn't it—it was *War in the Roses* or something like that. The husband and wife was *battling*, Max, I'm talking outright war, and she got stuck in the chandelier, and it crashed down on—"

"Didn't see it, Aisha. I was on lockdown for six long ones."

"Six years?! How old are you?"

"Twenty-seven."

"Well, you sure look good for your age. Anyway, I was *dying*, that movie was mad wak!"

Max rubbed his hand over his smooth head. "So how you get tripped up in this patrol madness anyway?"

She liked his calm, low voice. "Like all of us, I guess. Hated school, had babies, collected checks, and chilled. Then all of a sudden the party was over. And since I ain't no outdoor maid to be washin' or sweepin'—here I am. How 'bout you?"

"Different road, same dead end. Had a kid, messed with drugs, grand larceny, got locked up, and the mother split. I'm clean now, but there wasn't no 'parolees wanted' signs out here. Me and my son had to eat, so we went on assistance, and five years later here I am. Back in the days I wanted to be a cop. Guess this about as close to the police force as a brother like me gets."

A knee bumped against Aisha's shoulder. "*Excuse* me, miss, you are *blocking* the—"

Aisha was on her feet in a second. "Lady, you crazy?!" she shouted.

Max grabbed her hard by the arm. "Let it go, sister. We not out here for that, and you don't want no beef with the police your first day out."

Aisha tried to break from his grasp, but he held on. She yelled, "You *betta* run . . ."

Max couldn't help laughing with Aisha as the blonde flew down the marble steps and fought through the crowd as if she had a pit bull at her heels.

"You young sisters are fierce! Y'all ready in a flash to go toe-to-toe, blow for blow. What happened to sugar and spice and everything nice?"

"That don't apply to us. Nobody respect project girls until we kick they butt. Then they still don't. But at least we kicked they butt."

Max said, "Come on, Iron Mike, we *supposed* to be on patrol. And we *are* blocking the stairs."

They strolled the west balcony, then along the east balcony and down the broad staircase to the vast concourse. Through the dining concourse they wandered, past store windows, fast-food spots, and newsstands. Down in the subway, people called to each other, patrollers' walkie-talkies crackled, and trains screeched and squealed. A distinguished-looking gray-haired man in a designer business suit asked Aisha how to get to the Chrysler Building.

"By going up them steps to the middle of the terminal where they got that big clock with the four sides and asking the information lady. I ain't from around here."

"But I've asked you. You *are*, are you not, part of the terminal staff? I'm not from around here either. I'm English, and I need to get to the Chrysler Building right away. Now will you help me, or shall I have to speak to your supervisor?"

"Uh-oh," said Max.

"Boy, I could care less if you English, Amish, Polish, or a goddamn knish. Do this cap say 'Information Booth'? I'm a cop, Sherlock, so git out my face before I hafta spray you with Mace!"

The Englishman turned white, pink, then deep red. "Please pardon me, officer, I thought—" He dashed off in the direction of the stairs.

"Like whoa, Max, you saw that?! He gave me *mad* props, I'm talking R-E-S-P-E-C-T. I *like* this patrol thing. SYP got *juice*!"

"Threatening to bust out the Mace will definitely get you

a kind of respect, Aisha. In the joint, the wakkest dude gets props too, the one who'll stab a brother for a pack of smokes or beat down a guard to prove his manhood. But what goes around comes around. And I seen brothers come back from ten days in the hole completely broke down."

"Well, that's *they* problem. All I know is, today I got the *power*."

They continued on their patrol, turning down a walkway leading to the lower level. A guy in sunglasses with a checkered doo-rag on his head was hanging out near the public restrooms, taking long draws on a cigarette. Max identified himself as a patroller and told the kid that smoking wasn't allowed in the terminal.

"Step, sucka," he sneered.

"Hey brother, I'm just—"

"I ain'tcha brother, sucka." The teenager patted a bulge under his sweatshirt and lowered his voice. "I *said* step. You interfering in my business, ah-ight? Now step, or your freak"—he winked at Aisha—"gon' be lookin' through a donut in your chest."

Max stepped back. "Cool, man. Just doing my job. But it's cool, you the man."

Within seconds, Aisha and Max were up the staircase and standing in a swirl of people in the middle of the concourse. Aisha's chest heaved up and down, her breathing heavy. Max draped his arm around her shoulders.

"Max, I have two children at home, and that thug was ready to start shooting!" She flipped on her walkie-talkie.

"He's just a punk," said Max. "Don't call it in. These cops out here will swarm that brother like an army and take him down on sight."

"But he woulda shot *you*—and probably me too!"

"No, he wouldn't have—he was frontin', trust me. I wasted six years of my life with dudes like him. There's too many of us behind bars. We can't play into their system, Aisha."

Aisha still wanted to call Mrs. Vinker. "Well, it ain't like they didn't *do* nothin' to end up where they at." She was pissed off.

Max sighed. "It's deeper than that, sister."

She gave him the "whatever" look and walked away. She went down the sloping passage leading to the subway trains. Sticking the SYP cap into a bag, she clicked off her walkie-talkie and waited for the Brooklyn-bound train, keeping a nervous eye out.

Louise was at one end of the sofa flipping through a newspaper with her grandchildren napping at the other.

"You home early, it ain't even three. Did y'all already catch that Grand Central slasher?"

"I didn't catch nothin' but rude people's attitude. And a wannabe gangsta flashing a gun."

"Lord have mercy!"

"I ain't cut out for this cop stuff, Ma, even if it's fake— too many gangsta wannabes in New York. And guess who the supervisor is? Miss Vinker! She can't stand me, so I know she gon' be real happy to fire my behind."

"Nothing's worth getting yourself hurt. But look at them two sleeping beauties. How you gonna quit?"

Aisha leaned over and gave each one a kiss. She then did something that made Louise flinch, it was so unusual—she kissed her too. "Love you, Ma."

Louise looked down. "Me too. Be careful."

Almost three o'clock. School would be out soon, and Aisha really needed to talk to her girls.

"Keeba and Teesha here?"

Mrs. Washington handed Aisha a flyer. "Yes indeed, they came in the door a few minutes ago." Her powerful voice boomed through the apartment. "Kee! Tee! Aisha's here!" She pointed to the flyer. "This coming Friday a group of us are going to the Newark Tabernacle of the Holy Gospel Pentecost for a weekend gospel fund-raiser. My two always seem to have some important test to study for every time a nice event like this is going on. But why don't you come— and bring your little ones, get them started early in the way of the Lord."

Aisha coughed, cleared her throat, and glanced down the hallway. What was taking them so long? "It sound good, Miss Washington, but I'ma be sort of busy with—"

Screams and shouts. "Aaarrrgh, it's the po-lice!!! Shut the door, Mommy!" yelled Teesha.

"Hurry up!" hollered Keeba. "Officer Ai gon' pistol-whip us for littering her subway."

They bustled past their mother and started pushing against the door.

Aisha burst out laughing, pushing back from the other side. "You have the right to remain ghetto and wild like y'all is, and anything you say can and will make me smack you!"

Two against one, they shoved on the door, back and forth, it nearly closing, then swinging open, slamming shut, banging open.

"If you hellions break my door! Keeba! Teesha! Aisha!" Mrs. Washington tugged her daughters by their sweatshirts. "I'm not playing—you gonna break my damn door!"

"Oooooh, Mommy said the D word!" screamed Keeba, and raced to her room.

Teesha ran behind her sister, laughing, "You in big trouble now, Sister Washington!"

Aisha followed, knocking over a chair on her way.

All three leaped onto the bed and shrieked as it made a loud crack. Each blamed the other for breaking the bed with her "two-ton booty," and the girls tried to kick one another onto the floor. Gasping, panting, and laughing, they slowly caught their breath and settled down.

The sisters teamed up.

"Why you gots to be wildin' in our crib?"

Keeba said, "Yeah, makin' our poor mama curse, and she

tryin' so hard to git to Heaven. Girl, we gon' PARTAAAAYY this weekend!"

"Shhh, Keeba, she right in the kitchen," whispered Teesha. "So how many you bust on your first day as a cop, Ai?"

Aisha recounted her day as a patroller.

They kept interrupting Aisha's story.

"Gurrlll!"

"That's drama!"

"No, she *didn't*!"

"All I know is, I ain't gettin' killed for no dollar-a-hour fake workfare gig. I cut out early today 'cause of what happened, but I'ma talk to Miss Vinker tomorrow about doing a different job."

Keeba said, "But ain't nothin' left but all that scrubbin' and cleanin', and you said you wasn't goin' there."

"True dat," said Aisha, shaking her head. "I don't know, I hafta figure out something. In the meantime, what y'all got in the refrigerator to settle my nerves?"

sixteen

Mrs. Vinker glanced at her watch as Aisha came running toward the group the next day. Seven fifty-six. "You cutting it close, Ingram. Is your son better?" A look of worry flashed in the supervisor's eyes for a second. Aisha stared, sleepy and sweating.

"Yeah, how *is* the little brother?" asked Max. "When your moms beeped me with that message about him having a hundred three temperature, I knew it was serious."

Aisha looked at Max. She didn't get it. Then she got it. "He a little better. We took him to the emergency room 'cause he was throwing up and diarrhea was—"

"We don't need the details. Next time you have a family emergency, and this goes for all of you, I better get a call *before* you go gallivanting off. Now circulate. Yesterday was quiet —let's hope for the same today. Ingram, put your cap on."

Aisha and Max agreed it might be better to stay away

from the main terminal and just patrol the subway platforms and entrances.

"I owe you, Max. At first, I was like, 'What is he talkin' about, nothin' wrong with my baby.' Thanks."

He shrugged. "Ain't no thang to help a sister out. Our little encounter of the homeboy kind shook you up, I can understand that. But thank *you* for letting it go. Man, I couldn't have nothing like that on my conscience. Enough there already."

"Ah-ight. It's all good."

The second morning was a replay of the first, noisy and hectic. The 4 and 5 express trains screeched into the station one after another and people charged across the platform to the number 6 local, using their elbows and shoulders like running backs. Tourists wearing golf clothes, fanny packs, and cameras huddled around a guide.

Aisha bought a bag of Cheez Doodles and a pack of Chuckles at a newsstand. Max, orange juice in hand, made fun of her diet. They walked the length of platforms, sat on benches, climbed stairs, inspected exits. A photography exhibition in Vanderbilt Hall kept their attention for a good half hour. At the Lexington and 43rd Street entrance a bunch of kids wearing identical T-shirts from some private school jumped the turnstile. They froze and turned pink as Aisha and Max approached.

"Uh-oh, guys, undercover cops," someone whispered.

Max put on his tough cop voice. "What's going on here?! Don't tell me you rich kids can't afford a token."

A long-haired girl with five earrings in each ear spoke. She looked pleadingly at Aisha. "Excuse us, officers, we're er—late for our finals and didn't have time to—"

Aisha held her hand in front of the girl's face. "Talk to the hand. Now, how y'all didn't have time to buy tokens when there ain't even no line at the booth? I should bust y'all just for thinking we stupid enough to believe that 'cause we black."

"Oh God, no, that is *so* not anything I would ever think. Ask any of these guys, they know me and what I stand for. I am *so* not about race!"

"Well, I *is*. So you got two minutes to *race* right over to that token booth and pay your fare, or y'all's gettin' cuffed."

The teens scrambled back under the turnstile, calling over their shoulders, "Thanks, you guys are so right on!" As soon as the kids were out of sight, Aisha and Max cracked up.

There was a pizza break, followed by more patrols. The station's after-lunch pace was slow, and the riding public had thinned out. They followed the signs to the shuttle passage. A violinist had set up near the shuttle line and was playing a sweet adagio. Tired of walking, Max leaned on a railing, and Aisha sat on a crate munching a cherry-flavored Chuckle. The doors of the short shuttle train opened. From the car emerged a smartly dressed, shapely woman who towered head and shoulders above the other passengers. Aisha had just popped the licorice Chuckle, her favorite, into her mouth and was savoring it with closed eyes. Satisfied, she slowly opened her eyes and looked directly into the woman's. Debbie Silver was striding toward her so deliberately that Aisha tensed up as if she was going to have to throw down, this time in self-defense.

"Aisha!"

Aisha jumped to her feet. Max eyed the woman from head to toe and back up again.

"Aisha!"

"Miss Silver, *she* the one who—"

"I know, I know. She'd given away your slot a whole half hour early. Pammie's history. Gone. But why didn't you call to clear things up? There's been some interest, but your file was missing—Pammie no doubt—and for the life of me, I could *not* remember your last name! I'm so glad to see you. The timing is perfect too, because I'm just out of a meeting."

Aisha was beaming. "Max! Come meet my friend Debbie Silver. She a model!" She introduced them, but her mind was on one thing. "What kinda interest? You mean I got a modeling job?!" She started dancing and waving her arms in the air.

Debbie Silver took Aisha by the arm. "Slow down, star! No, it's not modeling. It's a job I think you'll like even more. Can you skate?"

Debbie invited them both for coffee. Max didn't want any beefs with Mrs. Vinker and turned the woman down, but he offered to cover for Aisha. Aisha and Debbie went together to the Park Avenue Coffee Shop, and an hour later, her head full of fantasy and excitement, Aisha floated home to Brooklyn.

The pounding at the door rattled the kitchen dishes. "Who in the hell . . ." said Louise. "*Coming*, dammit, and something *better* be on fire."

Aisha burst into the apartment jumping up and down, cheering and shaking her butt.

"Ma! I'ma be a model! I mean, a actress! We gon' get *paid*, Ma, at last." Louise made her daughter sit down and explain what the devil was going on.

"First, me and Max had messed with these white kids for fun, then we was patrolling near the Grand Central shuttle. So I was eating Chuckles, you know how much I love them, especially the black one I always save for last, and who do I see but the lady from the model agency! Debbie Silver! She is *down*, Ma! She got me on a TV commercial for this skating joint that this rap label and a Rollerblade company is hookin' up. They gon' open all these rinks all over the place! I'ma be the project girl of the world!"

Louise's mouth was open. She was happy and shocked and hardly understanding anything Aisha was saying through that mouth of hers going ninety miles an hour.

"It is so phat! They need a girl from every race, like in them Benetton ads, and I'm the black one! And ya *know* dat 'cause I'm *black* like dat!" She was doing a booty dance and giggling. "I get big *bling, bling* cash up front and zidjewels every time it be on TV. So they can keep their welfare and workfare and stick they check where the sun don't shine!"

Louise was all smiles, blinking like she was waking up from a dream. Then she asked, "What you call the jewels they gonna pay you in?"

The beats and bass were bouncing off the walls of the production studio, and Missy's voice gliding and smooth sliding, growling and purring. The good-looking commercial director, all eyes and height and loafers without socks, was freaking out.

"Girls! Girls!" he shouted, clapping his hands twice. "I do not want to hear that the blades don't fit! Jam those feet in—they're not Cinderella's slippers! Your residuals will buy you all the blister treatments you'll ever need! The ramp ready? I need that ramp!"

The final hammering was being done on the wooden Y-shaped slope designed to propel the skaters directly toward, then immediately to both sides of, the camera.

"Amanda! Paulanne! You're on the right." The two girls rolled onto the large X's marked "Latina" and "White."

"Okay, that's great. Ginny and Sonya, you're over there." He gestured toward the "Asian" and "Native" floor markers. "Let's go, let's go. Sound people, is the rap cued up? Time is money. Where's Aisha? Get Aisha out here!"

Inside the skaters' makeshift dressing room, Aisha, wobbly and shaky, was trying to balance on her Rollerblades.

Her hair was styled in a loose pageboy, and her face and eyes were fully made up. She was beautiful. And frustrated.

"I can't even stand up on these things—how I'm s'pose to roll around on 'em? I ain't no ice skater. Y'all gon' have to get me normal skates."

The production assistant, a fair young woman with a mass of tangled red hair, was holding Aisha up by the elbows and talking into her telephone headset. The director's voice came back so loud that it reached her in stereo.

"I don't care if you put remote control cars on her feet, Valerie, just roll her out here!"

The assistant ran from the dressing room and returned within minutes, pale and panting, carrying a box. "Hurry, Aisha, Peter's going *Sturm und Drang.*"

Aisha put on the white leather shoe skates and sailed onto the ramp.

"Why, thank you, Miss Ingram!" said Peter, directing Aisha to the "Black" marker in the center. "The shot's from the waist up anyway, so the Bomb Blades people won't know a *thing*. Let's hit it, people!"

The skaters, wearing matching HOUSE OF RAP 'N ROLL sweatshirts overhanging baggy jeans, rolled together down the ramp and split off in pairs, leaving Aisha to head straight to the camera, spin to a stop, and say, "Rap 'n Roll New York in the house!" Take after take, the girls rolled and split apart, again and again, until all five were complaining about sore feet. Aisha was getting grouchy.

"I'm tired! What you trying to get to? All we doing is the same thing over and over."

The other skaters agreed, adding their own individual complaints about cramps and hunger and having to pee.

"What I'm trying to get to, Miss Ingram, is perfection. That and nothing less is expected by clients who pay top dollar for our services. Ginny's timing is still a little fuzzy, and I need to see joy radiating from your lovely black face because you're essentially the It Girl on this shoot. Now stop bitching, and give me take eighteen!"

Aisha felt like she could give him a good whack upside the head but thought back to the BIGMODELS receptionist. No, she was done fighting like that. Now she had to fight the fatigue in her legs and the urge to stick her tongue out at the camera. Doing commercials was hard work, not like it seemed on TV. She wondered how many takes Debbie Silver had gone through before she had tossed her hair and turned on her foot exactly the way they wanted her to.

"Time's money, Miss Ingram, and we're waiting!"

Aisha took a deep breath and skated back to her X. She skated and smiled and said "Rap 'n Roll New York in the house!" so many times that she became giddy. The other girls did too, and after a while they were laughing so much, the makeup artist had to keep touching up their tear-streaked faces. Aisha messed up a couple times and said "Nappy Roll," which only made them more giddy.

On take twenty-five, Ginny crashed into Amanda, and both girls landed on their butts. Seeing Peter roll his eyes and suck his teeth, something Aisha didn't know white people did, almost made her lose it. She rolled toward the camera fighting the urge to bust out laughing. With a giant smile on her face and too wrecked to care, she sang out, "Rap 'n Roll New York in the house, y'all!"

Peter shrieked. "That's it! I love the 'y'all' at the end, Aisha! So urban, so ethnic, so perfect!" The skaters tumbled in a heap onto the floor moaning. The crew applauded.

seventeen

Aisha became an instant star. Not only because she rolled into living rooms across New York beaming a happy smile but because she got free T-shirts and Rollerblades for her friends. Toya, Keeba, and Teesha mastered their blades in a week—even Starlett cruised around the projects on blades—while Aisha stuck to her four-wheelers, troubled only by the need to choose which of her ten pairs to wear with which color outfit. Without depriving themselves of one bite of their favorite foods, they all began slimming down because they skated everywhere—school, church, supermarkets, movies, even across the Brooklyn Bridge to J&R Music World, where the cashiers greeted Aisha like a celebrity.

"You the Rap n' Roll girl, right?! Whoa, like I been doing blades since they first came out! Hook me up on TV!"

Raven called from college. She nearly passed out, up late

studying with the TV on, when she saw Aisha grinning at her. "I thought for a minute, Ai, that I was hallucinating. I couldn't believe it! My suite mates were ready to kill me for waking them up screaming 'That's my girl! That's Ai!' "

Max, who was spending a lot of time with Aisha, insisted he was too old to do skates or blades. She was really into him but was "staying focused," as Debbie Silver suggested, on keeping her flow.

Even Kevin tried to make a comeback.

"Yeah, Ai, it's me, Kev. Just thought I'd give you a shout, you know, kick it with you a little bit, say wassup. Everybody giving you mad props for the TV thing, baby, and that make me feel real good, seeing that we—"

Aisha was stretched out on the living room couch, playing with her DVD remote control.

"What? Since when *we* anything at all? What happened to Blondie?"

"Aw, man, she the past, baby."

"Well, that make two of y'all. Gotta go. 'Bye."

When Louis Jr. and Luis Jr. called all excited from Florida, they put their boss on, who just had to say hello to "the boys' " famous sister. He was putting together a publicity budget, he said, and wanted to "brainstorm" with her, when she had the time of course, about young, hip ways to promote his Doubletake chain. Maybe she and the kids could vacation in the Keys, at the condo.

Aisha didn't know she could feel so much power. And not from kicking butts but just from making good things happen for herself. She'd finally gotten the break she needed, and this time she hadn't blown it.

The House of Rap 'n Roll people were thrilled with the public's response to the commercial and called Debbie Silver whenever they wanted to open a new rink in what they called a "homegirl demographic" area. Aisha taped spots for rinks in Philadelphia, Washington, D.C., Trenton, and Hartford, and the company was planning to expand westward. She opened a savings account and watched in amazement as it filled with residual payments, even when she wasn't working. Louise had no more trouble making rent payments. Aisha had found a place for herself and the kids and had already packed a few things in boxes.

One evening Aisha's cell phone rang. She checked the Caller ID but didn't recognize the number.

She answered with her usual "Ai in the house, wassup?"

The caller laughed. "Still working?"

Aisha was puzzled. "Who this?"

"It's me, Ebony. Why didn't you call me back?"

Ebony? Call her back?

"Ebony, hey! You saw my commercial?! I can get you some Rollerblades if you want. But what you mean I didn't call you back? You never called *me* back!"

"Aisha, I returned your call a couple days after you left that first message months ago, and again when I saw you on TV. I thought you were being *all that* and didn't want to be bothered. I am *so* proud of you, girl, you have no idea. Didn't Louise tell you? She promised she would."

Now Aisha was downright confused. "Nope, she never said nothing, Ebbie. You know I wouldn't diss you like that."

"Hold it, Ai! Just because you're rich and famous doesn't mean you can call me Ebbie. You know I *hate* that name. Anyway, Miss Rock and Roll—"

"*Rap*, Ebony—"

"Pardon *me*. Miss *Rap* and Roll."

"Rap'n Roll—"

"Aisha!"

They had the same laugh, and it filled both homes. Ebony was the first to compose herself.

"As I was *saying*, Frank and I would love to have you over to the house this coming weekend. Bring Starlett and Ty too. I *told* Louise to tell you. Put her on—and we'll see you Saturday. *In the house.*"

Louise was sitting on the bed brushing her hair and humming to the radio. She smiled.

"Who is it?"

Aisha handed her the phone.

"Hello?" She waved Aisha from her room.

Aisha decided, after looking at a street map, not to skate to Astoria. The N train would do just fine. She got off at Astoria Boulevard and followed the directions scribbled on the back of her "Aisha Ingram—Actress, Model, Dancer" business card. A few blocks later, she was standing at the door of a modest one-level home in the middle of a street of attached houses. She smoothed down her ponytail, adjusted her sunglasses, and pressed the buzzer.

"Aisha!" The sisters hugged. Aisha came up to Ebony's shoulder. Height was the most obvious physical difference between them. Along with her thick hair and high cheekbones, what really distinguished Ebony from Aisha were her pale, almost gray eyes.

"You look *good*, kid. But no, you do *not* have on shades as cloudy as it is! Come on in, Miss Thing, Frank's in the kitchen. Hey, where're the kids?"

Louise had taken them to the Prospect Park Zoo.

"Really? Is that . . . safe?"

"Uh-huh. She not drinking no more." Aisha felt proud saying that, like she had something to do with it.

Ebony nodded. "That's good—that's real good."

They walked into the small, curtained living room just as Frank was coming through the swinging kitchen doors carrying a tray with sandwiches and sodas. Aisha had only seen him in photos. He was as tall as Ebony, with broad shoulders, a thick chest, and thinning hair. *Cute though*, she thought, trying to imagine them kissing.

"So you're the family celebrity! Good to meet you, Aisha," he said, shaking her hand. "Heard nice things about you."

Aisha had a million questions: how Ebony got into being a probation officer, why Frank became a cop, what made Ebony move out the projects, if they liked each other as soon as they met . . .

"Whoa, slow down!" exclaimed Frank. "Maybe you can help me interrogate perps when you're not making commercials."

"What's a perps?"

Ebony laughed. "That's cop shop talk for *perpetrators*, Aisha." She explained how the boys had driven her nuts when she was little with their constant teasing and taunting.

"With Daddy always gone and Mom totally into the twins, I felt dissed and got mad. When a *new* baby girl was suddenly arriving on the scene—you—I felt like I was being replaced, so I split pretty fast. Joined the Job Corps, where I met this Irish cop guy"—she winked at her husband—"and that's about it. The PO thing is just about liking kids and trying to keep them out of trouble while they're on probation." She glanced at Frank. "From a comfortable distance."

Aisha told them about herself—dropping out, Kevin, having kids, trying to stay on welfare. The story about Nurse Constantino made Frank turn red from laughing. "I gotta give it to you, kid, you got heart!"

"That's what Debbie always say."

Ebony wanted to know all about Debbie Silver and BIG-MODELS. "You know, Ai, when I was a teenager, I tried to get into modeling, even went to a couple of agencies. But back then a black girl had to look like a beige white girl. They said my look was too 'exotic.' "

"Fools," said Frank, clearing the table.

"It's cool though. I was too immature to have big money and sudden celebrity. Probably would've got caught up in some bad stuff. Now *you*, you seem to be wearing *being all that and more* quite well. But you know, Ai, you can't skate forever. At some point, you might need a skill to fall back on, unless of course, you *really* blow up. Frank's brother just opened a computer training academy. You get a nine-month training course and can even do a lot of the work from home. Why not check it out? It might come in handy down the road."

Aisha said she would. "But you *know* I'ma be blowin' it up. Debbie got me a regular commercial where I don't be skating. I smile at some kinda diet pepper steak I get out the microwave and be like, 'Why just do chicken right when you got Chinese lite?' "

Ebony frowned.

Aisha laughed. "Whatever. At least nobody can cut off my zidjewels."

Aisha got home late. Louise was still up. They'd all had a good time at the zoo. Aisha talked with excitement about her visit to Queens and how she felt so close to her sister.

"How come you ain't told me about Ebony calling?"

Louise heaved a long sigh and looked down.

"I don't know what to say . . . your mother's a scared old fool."

"You ain't old."

"I'm fifty years old, Aisha."

"Fifty? I thought you was a hundred." Aisha chuckled. She knew exactly how old her mother was.

Louise continued. "I was afraid Ebbie was gonna take you and the children away . . . put y'all up in her big house . . . and I'd be left here alone with nothing . . ." Tears filled her eyes.

Aisha stared, not knowing what to do. She had never seen her mother cry, although a couple times she thought she'd heard . . . sounds.

"But Ma," she said quietly, "*you* was the one who said—"

"That was just drunk talk, baby. I love you . . . the children . . . this family already broke up enough. I woulda never . . ." She was too choked up to go on.

They sat in silence.

The next morning Aisha was up early. Starlett had awakened her climbing into her bed. No matter what she did, Aisha couldn't get her daughter used to her own bed. Without fail, Starlett would find her way, sometimes sound asleep, to her mommy.

Noises awoke Louise. She went to the living room. Aisha was humming, surrounded by boxes. Clothes, toys, sneakers, CDs, and skates covered the floor.

"Ai, what in heaven's name are you doing at this hour?" asked Louise, rubbing her eyes.

"Unpacking."

A smile spread across Louise's face. Aisha and her mother stood together hugging for a long time.

GAYLORD RG